Third publishing by Amazon
Text and images copyright Ric

Special Thanks

J. Wang
Brent Hinkins
Paul Brasch
Leah Bateman

HIGHWAY HUNTER

Written by Richard Chappell

Illustrated by J.Wang

Chapter 1

The Biggest Predator Wins

The sun sets in the iron red Australian outback. A large, green lizard stands still with his head upright on a large red rock. A crow circles ominously above and the lizard scurries away.

A lone electric campervan cruises on a desert highway. Anti-coal, pro-vegan, and conserve the land stickers adhere to its back window, a rolling advertisement for climate change propaganda.

Inside the campervan the supple feet of twenty something carefree traveler, Helen, rest on the dash. Her legs are lovely, lean and tanned and seem to go on forever before reaching her frayed denim cutoff pants. Helen wears a tight white singlet that shows off her considerable assets. Paul, Helen's hipster boyfriend is driving.

A dirty, red v8 Ute with a "HURRY UP" sign welded to the bonnet tears up behind the campervan. Paul slides Helen's heels off the dash. The Ute's overbearing steel bull bar screams up behind the campervan to intimidate its occupants. The Ute driver has Paul and Helen's full attention. The Ute floodlights flash into Paul's eyes, temporarily blinding his vision of the road ahead.

Inside the v8 Ute, three teenage boys fired up on youthful testosterone are out to wreak havoc. Matt and Joe are in the cab, while Trev stands on the flatbed tray. Matt drives the Ute and he is thirsty for adrenalin charged activities. On the cusp of adulthood, Matt's recent escapades include smashing down mailboxes at the local retirement village and revving the v8 engine of his Ute through the suburban streets in the wee hours of the morning.

Joe is a skinny meth-head and Matt's number two. Trevor, the wild one, screams from the flatbed tray like a lunatic. The end of Joe's glass meth pipe glows red. Joe's distinct lack of intelligence is of little use to Matt, but he is good for a laugh. Matt takes the pipe off Joe. Joe is so fried that he goes through the motion of inhaling even though the pipe is no longer in his hands.

"Hang on fucker!" Matt hollers. Matt drags on the pipe and passes it to Trev.

Trevor fills his lungs with the smoke. The meth runs through his body powering his ADHD madness. He bangs on the roof of the Ute and yells, "Faster, Faster, Faster!"

Joe puts his hand out the window and Trev passes him the glass pipe. Matt smiles as he closes in on Paul and Helen's campervan. His smile turns sweet and nasty as the steel bull bar sparks on the campervan.

Matt shouts, "Pull over you greenie fucker so I can bang your missus!"

In the campervan, the road is screaming past Paul's peripheral vision while his eyes are dead set on the rearview mirror and the occupants of the Ute. Helen now sits bang upright with her legs tightly clenched together. Sweat starts to soil her pretty, little cutoffs.

Paul gripes, "Bloody nutcase meth heads! Could you get any closer to our ass you fuckers?"

"Can't you go any faster?" Helen mutters.

Paul "No darling. We're battery powered."

"But…" Helen nags.

Paul interjects, “Go electric you said… it’ll be better for the environment you said!”

The Ute bull bar bumps into the back of the campervan.

Helen screams, “Jesus! They're lunatics!”

Matt and Joe turn to each other and smile with malicious intent as Matt floors it. The v8 Ute bumps hard into the back of the van and the bull bar becomes lodged in the van’s rear bumper, interlocking the two vehicles together. Paul and Helen are up shit creek. Matt, Joe and Trevor celebrate as Matt steers the interlocked vehicles down the highway.

Matt hollers, “How do you like that, fuckers?”

Joe cheerleads, “Keep it up Matty!”

Trevor’s fists nearly take the cab roof off as he howls like a crazed wolf. Matt turns the steering wheel left and right, and the campervan dislodges from the Ute bull bar. Paul looks with satisfaction into the rear-view mirror, but the Ute stays hard up their ass. Suddenly, a big red kangaroo bounces onto the highway in front of the campervan.

Helen screams, “Lookout!”

Paul is in the zone, and he reacts swiftly. He pulls the steering wheel hard left to avoid hitting the kangaroo. Helen shrieks. Paul locks eyes with the kangaroo briefly before it bounces out of his line of sight. The campervan skids off the highway and spins around 360 degrees in the gravel before it bursts a steer tire and becomes airborne. The campervan flips multiple times, bashing it up and throwing debris inside everywhere.

The Ute is barreling down with a force too great to avoid the kangaroo. Matt has no time to change direction, his attention distracted by his need for the pipe. The bull bar slams hard into the kangaroo, killing it instantly and stopping the forward momentum of the Ute.

The impact causes Trevor to slam his abdomen into the cab of the Ute. He gets winded and keels over as he tries to regain his breath. The collision causes Joe to smash the meth pipe into his face. Pieces of the glass pipe pierce his face and become lodged into his cheek. Joe reaches for his face and screams out in pain.

Joe shouts “Fuck! My face!”

Matt looks over to see the broken glass fragments lodged in Joe’s face with blood pouring out.

Matt shouts, “You idiot Joe! You’ve broken the pipe!”

Joe cries out, “What about my face man? This is your fault!”

Matt is not accustomed to Joe challenging him. He responds by pulling a broken glass fragment out of Joe’s face.
Joe screams “Aagh!” as blood pours down his cheek.
Matt says, “It’s not my fault you’re a fucking idiot Joe”.
Paul and Helen's campervan lies in a crumpled mess behind on the gravel.

The Ute has taken a significant hit. It is still running but not as well and with significant damage to the front end. Smoke escapes from under the bonnet. Matt, Joe, and Trevor are not the only ones on the hunt.

A mint condition, black semitrailer powers at high speed past the scene of the campervan wreck. Camouflaged by darkness, the black semi ejects flames and smoke from two chrome vertical exhausts.

Alice, 45 years old, drives the truck that has an insignia on the grill reading '**BEAST**'. Alice has long black hair, dark tinted glasses, black jacket over a singlet, black jeans and black boots. He is a powerfully built man with a large, bulky frame. Heavy metal rock music blares from the stereo. As the surroundings turn dark Alice takes off his sunglasses. He is no stranger to the dark; it is where he feels most at home.

The 'Beast' is Alice's home. In the back of the truck cab there is a sleeper, fridge, cooktop and laptop, all the essentials for Alice's day-to-day life. Alice has called the Beast his home for many years. And he is very satisfied with his life. A glass box with a human foot bone fully intact is screwed on top of the front dash.

The Beast roars down the highway. Condensation drips from the diesel-powered refrigeration unit on the front of the trailer. The motor elicits a gentle hum and keeps the internal contents of the trailer cold.

In the driver cab Alice soothes the Beast. "Come on girl, we want to run smooth and wet," he says. There is a Control Panel linked to an internal computer adjacent to the steering wheel. The control panel is comprised of many buttons which all serve various functions for Alice to carry out his torturous deeds. He has a computer nerd to thank for that one. Alice dispatched with him once his usefulness had been fulfilled.

Alice is on the prowl for something to appease his appetite for destruction. He finds it not far ahead in the form of Matt's Ute. The Beast's floodlights bathe the Ute as it closes in on its tail. A sinister smile comes across his face. He loves the thrill of the chase and the anticipation of what lies ahead.

Alice presses his foot down on the accelerator. Fire and black smoke blow out of the twin vertical exhaust pipes. The Beast taunts the little Ute, closing to within a whisker of its rear end. Alice takes his foot off the accelerator and the powerful engine brakes kick in which makes an intimidating engine roar. This temporarily backs the Beast away from its predatory grip on the Ute.

Matt, staring down the Beast in the rear-view mirror shouts, “Who does this motherfucker think he is. Take out the shotgun!”
Joe pulls a sawn-off shotgun out from underneath the seat. He passes it out the window to Trevor.

Trevor takes the shotgun, cocks the chamber, and says, “Time to turn this shit up a notch!”

Trevor aims at Alice and says, “Time to meet your maker, motherfucker!”

Alice looks on with a knowing smirk. These young boys have challenged the wrong man. Alice turns on the truck high beam lights. Trevor's sight is temporarily blinded. He raises his left arm to block out the lights. Alice accelerates the truck. The full power of the Beast's engine roars to life. Black smoke and fire blow out the exhaust as the front bull bar crashes into the back of the Ute.

Trevor squeezes the trigger. The shotgun fires into the darkness missing his intended target. The recoil causes Trevor to stumble and drop the shotgun off the back of the Ute and onto the road.

Trev shouts, "Shit!"

Matt shouts, "Trev? You bloody idiot!"

"Oh no," says Joe. "This guy ain't playin' around, Matt."

Matt snaps, "Shut the fuck up Joe!"

Trevor regains his composure just as the Beast accelerates again. Black smoke and fire blow out the twin vertical exhausts as the Beast slams into the back of the Ute again, this time disabling the power steering of the Ute. The powerful collision knocks Trev off the back of the Ute. The Beast rolls over Trevor's body like a speed bump, crushing and pulverising him into minced meat.

Joe screams, "Fuck me dead!"

"Ouch! That's gotta hurt!" Alice says with a wry smile.

The Beast accelerates alongside the passenger side of the Ute.

Joe shouts out, "Fuck, Matt! We're next!"

Matt huffs in a panic, “Chill out pissant!”

The Beast slams into the passenger side door of the Ute. Glass shards from the passenger window fly into Joe’s face, cutting into his face. Blood runs down Joe's face like a teenage girl’s period running down her leg in the shower.

Matt shouts, “Fuck! Fuck!”

Joe yells, “It’s game over bro’! Fuckin’ game over!”

Matt shouts, “Shut up Joe!”

Alice locks eyes with Matt. He exhales his murderous intent. Alice pulls the steering wheel hard into the Ute. The Beast slams into the side of the Ute for a second time. The bull bar demolishes the passenger side door, crushing Joe’s leg and pummelling his head into the doorframe.

The Ute skids off the highway, spins around and rolls onto its roof in the gravel. Matt is suspended upside down by the seat belt. Joe lay unconscious on the Ute ceiling, having not had a seatbelt on. The petrol tank is cracked open and fuel leaks into the main cab of the Ute. The smell of petrol arouses Matt’s attention.

The Beast comes to a loud screeching halt on the highway.

Matt unbuckles his seatbelt, falls onto the ceiling and looks over at Joe, who lays unconscious. Mustering all his strength, Matt pulls himself through the driver side window. His torso gets jammed in the opening. Matt looks over to the Beast and sees Alice shuffling towards him. Alice lights a cigarette, ready to deliver his final sentence. He takes a drag as he watches the stream of leaking petrol from the punctured Ute fuel tank come towards him.

“Nighty night” Alice says and flicks the cigarette into the stream of petrol.

Matt uses all his strength to force his torso through the window jam and clear of the ute. The fire runs quickly along the stream of petrol and engulfs the Ute in flames. Matt manages to crawl away to safety as the flames incinerate Joe.

The Ute explodes. A mushroom of fire races into the sky. Matt is clear of the explosion but feels the hot embers and explosive heat. He looks up and, terrified, sees Alice looking down on him. The bright flames illuminate Alice in a hellish red glow.

Alice, holding the hunting knife, says, “Justice awaits you”.

Matt gasps, “That’s my friend burning to death, you sick fuck!”

Alice kicks Matt in the side of the head with his artificial foot, knocking him unconscious.

Hours pass. It will be dawn soon. The Beast sits idly by the side of the highway in the darkness. In the darkness of the trailer, a sinister growl awakens Matt. He does not know how long he has been out for, but he knows he is in trouble. He is incapacitated and suspended from the ceiling. The smell of rot and death is in the air. An ominous growl taunts him from below. Matt looks down. Amidst the darkness the evil amber eyes of a dangerous predator circle beneath him.

Suddenly, bright lights are switched on in the trailer. Through swollen eyes Matt discovers that his wrists are restrained by steel cuffs attached to chains, which anchor to track rollers running along the ceiling of the trailer. Matt stands precariously on a rusty steel cage housing a hungry pit-bull that is ready to pounce. The pit-bull leaps up and its teeth tear at the threads on Matt's shoes.

Alice sits comfortably in the prime mover of the Beast. He turns on a CCTV monitor, which is mounted in the top corner of the windscreen. Vision of Matt suspended from the ceiling in the trailer comes through on the monitor.

Cameras are mounted at the front and the rear of the trailer. Matt moves and the cameras tracks his movements, sending the video feed back to the monitor in Alice's prime mover. Alice flicks between video feeds on the monitor via a control panel.

Alice holds a two-way radio, which connects to a speaker in the trailer. He says into the two-way, "Say hello to my little friend, Justice!"

The dog Justice barks ferociously.

"Fuck off!" Matt shouts.

"That's no way to approach Justice" Alice says.

"Burn in hell!" Matt shouts.

Alice says, "Let me introduce you to the Peacemaker"

Alice presses a button on the control panel. A one-meter-long sharp steel spike protrudes out from the headboard of the trailer. The spike points directly for the chest of Matt. A terrified Matt fights to pulls his hands free of the cuffs restraining his wrists.

Alice revs the engine. He says, “Wanna go for a ride?”

Matt says, “Fuck you!”

Alice accelerates the Beast up to speed, going through the gears. He brakes suddenly, causing Matt to slip off the wireframe cage and suspending loosely by the chains. He searches for a firm footing as he hangs from the ceiling.

The Beast approaches a steep incline in the road. Alice shifts the gear stick into a lower gear and presses his foot down on the accelerator. Fire and smoke blow out of the twin vertical exhaust as it powers up the hillside. Inside the trailer, Matt pulls at the chains. He timidly puts his right foot back on top of Justice's cage. Justice jumps up, barking and biting viciously at Matt’s foot. Matt balances precariously on the cage.

Matt shouts, “D’you want a piece of me cunt?”

As the truck goes over the peak of the hillside, smoke and fire blow out of the exhaust. Alice sits comfortably, smiling grimly as the Beast goes full tilt, gaining tremendous momentum down the steep decline.

At the bottom of the hill Alice grips firmly on the steering wheel and says through the two-way, “Get ready for a surprise!” He activates the truck and trailer brakes. The twenty-two-wheeler Beast brakes hard, burning rubber on the motorway.

Matt screams out, terrified, as the sudden break in forward momentum propels him towards his impending demise.

Matt's chest is impaled on the steel Peacemaker. The sharp spike spears him all the way through his chest cavity before exiting his back. Matt's lungs fill with blood. The life drains out of Matt's eyes as he takes his last breath. With animal instincts unbound, Justice barks hungrily from his cage. Drool hangs from his pink and black gums as he hungers eagerly for the fresh kill. In the prime mover Alice presses a button on the control panel. The electronic gate on Justice's cage opens with a buzz.

Alice says into the two-way, "Clean this bludger up, Justice! Everything but the head!"

Justice launches full speed at Matt's impaled body. The dog attacks viciously, his canine teeth tearing at Matt's legs. Justice rips Matt apart, shredding him from the steel spike, and then pulling so hard on one leg that Matt's arm rips off at the shoulder joint. Then Justice does similarly so to the other arm. Matt's torso and legs fall to the trailer floor. His arms dangle loosely from the chain restraints. Blood drips down from the end of Matt's arms where his shoulder has been dislodged. Justice feeds hungrily on Matt's flesh. Everything but Matt's head which is to be kept as a souvenir.

Chapter 2
Dead Calm

It is a beautiful summer's day on a quiet tree-lined suburban street. Magpies and miners battle for bush cockroaches.

A shiny new video-drone flies overhead. A pot-bellied, middle-aged man uses a whipper snipper to trim the edges of his front lawn. The man stops and waves to a middle-aged blonde woman whose breasts sag lower than her beagles' ears droop.

The drone moves across the street and follows a group of young kids who race their scooters and pushbikes. A brown mongrel dog follows them closely off lead. As the group approaches the two beagles, the dogs face off and bark at each other. The incessant barking sets off other dogs down the street and then the entire neighborhood.

The beagles pull hard at their restraints. The woman tries to hold them back, but it is of little use. She shouts, "Quiet! Quiet down!" and uses some hand gesture she learned at an over-priced doggy training school, without success. The woman loses control and shouts, "You naughty children! Put him on a leash!"

The joker in the group points to the fat kid. "Did you hear that? She wants us to put you on a leash," he says.

The eldest kid in the group whistles and the mongrel dog obediently comes to full attention at his heels.

The drone flies further down the block to a high set brick house, numbered 11. A lean, 35-year-old man named Johnny is cleaning his white cab-over Volvo truck, which is parked in the driveway. His chrome rims and hubcaps are sparkling clean. Johnny maintains himself like he keeps his truck – outwardly clean-shaven. Dressed in a singlet and footy shorts that display his strong physique, he is in good nick for a trucker.

Inside the garage there is a Kingswood utility, minus the engine, which is being reworked, and a white Mini. The Mini belongs to Nicole, Johnny's second wife. On the verandah of Johnny's high set brick house, his 5-year-old boy, Charlie, controls the video drone via his computer. He proudly wears his Marvel superhero t-shirt as he runs surveillance over the neighborhood.

It is routine for Charlie to do flybys with his video drone during Johnny's obsessive truck cleaning sessions. All Charlie wants is a little attention. He sports a mischievous grin as he swoops the drone down towards his dad, who polishes his truck, oblivious to the incoming drone. The drone flies to within arm's reach of Johnny and it startles him.

Johnny looks up to the verandah and waves his fist around, shouting, "Charlie! Quit it or I'll confiscate that thing!"

Charlie knows that his father's bark is worse than his bite. So, Charlie continues to fly the drone overhead.

Charlie's Mum, Nicole opens the sliding door to confront Charlie on the verandah. Ten years younger than Johnny, Nicole cuts a fine figure with slender body and olive complexion. Charlie is her greatest asset. Yet Nicole never wanted to have kids. After seeing her sister give birth, she decided that natural childbirth was something she never wanted to experience. But then she got pregnant with Charlie. And with Caesarean sections being readily available she was able to avoid the nasty pain and stretching associated with natural childbirth. Although she has never had a strong motherly instinct, Nicole has won the approval of her mother and her clique, who gather for morning coffee and gossip about the relative success of each other's children.

Out on the verandah, Nicole says, "Charlie, stop that if you don't want your father to confiscate it?"

Charlie replies, "Ok mum."

"It's a lovely day Charlie. Why don't you go outside and play with

Georgie?"

"In a minute, mum."

Charlie redirects the drone over the front fence away from his father and into the backyard.

Charlie's attention remains focused on the computer and directing the drone. Nicole goes back inside and walks down the hallway to her stepdaughter Anna's bedroom. The door is shut with a 'PLEASE KNOCK' sign on it.

Anna, in between a young innocent girl and the lady she would become, sits at her desk studying from a large textbook. She wears a tight white singlet and skinny blue denim pants; Anna is very developed for her seventeen years. Her hourglass figure and large bosoms make Anna the envy of the other girls in her neighborhood. Anna has an explosive relationship with her stepmother Nicole. When Anna's mother was taken away to a psychiatric facility in Kruger because of drug addiction, Nicole offered Johnny a shoulder to cry on. Within a year Johnny divorced Anna's mum and Nicole took her place. Anna hates Nicole for ending her parent's relationship. The two of them clash, and with Johnny often away trucking, Anna's home life is volatile.

Nicole opens the door, walks inside, and says,

"Can you please do some chores around the house, young lady? This house is a mess, and the pool needs to be cleaned for Charlie's party tomorrow."

"Can't you knock?" Anna asks.

"We don't hide behind closed doors in this house. There are chores to be done, and you have to do your share."

"I've got no time. I'm studying for my finals."

"We've all got to contribute around here, young lady."

"I don't see Charlie contributing much."

"Charlie is just a little boy."

"Charlie gets whatever he wants."

"Don't be jealous of your brother."

"He's not my brother!" Anna replies.

"Sorry?"

"He's my half-brother"

"You keep that up and you'll be back living with your mother!"

"That'd suit me just fine…"

"Well, truth be known your junkie mum doesn't want you! So unfortunately, we're stuck with you…"

"Well, sorry Nicole but I have to study. So unfortunately, I can't help you with your chores."

"Very well. I don't know what you are going to be eating for dinner. You're a freeloader. Just like your mother. Take, take, take!"

"Shut up!"

"Lazy bitch!"

Nicole exits Anna's room leaving the door ajar. Anna gets up and closes the door. She returns to the desk, puts her headphones on and listens to her playlist. Music helps her to escape from her feelings of despair. Anna opens the picture gallery app on her mobile phone. She scrolls through the picture album of her family in happier times. Before her mother was struck down with anxiety and depression. The depression led to prescription drug use. Then her mum became addicted to the drugs that were supposed to help her. The break-up of her marriage to John followed. And this in turn led to a psychiatric illness and hospitalization. Anna loves her mum and wants to see her when she is doing better. But for now, she must work. Getting good results on her final exams will help her pursue her dream of studying medicine. So, Anna opens the mathematics textbook of algebra and continues to study.

Charlie flies the drone over Georgie, their fun-loving Labrador puppy. At eighteen months, Georgie is slowly progressing out of the naughty puppy stage. Georgie hates the drone and the buzzing noise it makes. He would like nothing more than to tear the drone into pieces. Georgie barks angrily at the drone. It is just out of his reach which is infuriating him. The gentle dog transforms into an angry mongrel when he is teased. An aggravated Georgie was responsible for destroying Charlie's last drone.

So, Charlie redirects the drone away from Georgie towards the pool. There is a gated fence around the pool. Nicole is sweeping the rubbish off the walls and into the center of the pool floor. There is a creepy crawly vacuuming the rubbish off the pool floor. Charlie flies the drone towards his mum Nicole. The drone flies close to the absentminded Nicole and startles her.

She gasps, and then sings out, “Charlie!”

Nicole swats at the drone with the pool sweeper, just missing it. Charlie smiles guiltily, having succeeded in scaring his mum.

With a disapproving grimace, she says sternly, “Put it away Charlie! That’s your final warning!”

Charlie does not put away the drone. Like his father, his mum delivers only empty threats. He is spoilt and he knows it. His mum will do nothing but ask him to put it away again at some later time.

The home phone rings. Nicole puts down the pool sweeper and returns to the house to take the call. In her hurry to get back to the house, Nicole inadvertently leaves the pool gate slightly ajar.

Charlie returns his attention to Georgie. He finds the puppy playing in the poolside sandpit.

Georgie sits chewing on a bone, relishing the treat, but he keeps an eye on the drone circling above. As the drone flies overhead, Georgie relaxes his grip on the bone. Once the drone is within striking distance, Georgie launches at it. Georgie catches the drone in his jaws and clamps down on it. Victory, Georgie thinks. Using his young canine instincts, Georgie shakes the drone vigorously.

On the verandah, Charlie shouts, “No Georgie!”

Charlie's computer screen turns black as Georgie breaks the video signal on the drone. Charlie runs down the stairs, out the back door and chases after Georgie, who has the drone firmly in his jaws. Georgie runs through the open gateway into the pool area with Charlie chasing him. Georgie runs around the outside of the pool with Charlie on his tail. As Charlie closes in on Georgie, Georgie evades capture by running around the corner of the pool and out of Charlie's reach.

Panicked, Charlie shouts out, "No Georgie! Bad dog! Drop it please…"

Georgie stops. He turns to face the boy. Georgie rests on his haunches, tightly gripping the drone whilst being wary of Charlie's movements. Charlie dives at Georgie. Georgie backs away, evading Charlie's attempt to catch him. Georgie runs away and the game continues.

Georgie runs around another corner of the pool and jumps over the pool sweeper, which Nicole left on the tiles. Charlie, running hard, trips on the pool sweeper and falls over. Charlie cracks his head on the edge of the tiles and falls into the pool unconscious. Georgie drops the drone and stands by the edge of the pool. Charlie lay face down in the pool with blood pooling around his head. Georgie barks loudly to get the attention of Johnny and Nicole.

Inside the house, Nicole is talking to her mum on the phone, showing off her latest purchase, "Look mum, new whisky glasses"

Nicole's mum responds, "When did you and Johnny begin drinking whisky?"

Nicole says, "Well, we can't be caught only drinking beer, can we?"

Georgie's barking increases in intensity.

Nicole's mum asks, "Nicole, what's the matter with Georgie?"

Nicole replies, "Who knows with that mutt? If it's not the possums, it's the dog next door or the cat across the road!"

"I'm glad you're not my neighbor," Nicole's mum responds.

"We have a collar that shocks the dog when it barks but Johnny thinks that's cruel," Nicole says, before continuing, "Anyhow mum, Johnny is driving interstate next week for work and I have a lady's lunch on Wednesday, so if you could look after Charlie, I'd really appreciate it… you're so good with him."

"What about Anna? Can't she look after Charlie?" Nicole's mum asks.

"Anna can't be relied on to do anything" Nicole responds.

Meanwhile Johnny, now filling the engine oil in his truck, becomes concerned at the intensity of Georgie's barking. Johnny drops what he is doing and hurries out to the backyard.

Johnny's eyes open wide in sheer terror when he sees Charlie face down in the pool with blood pooling around his head.

“No!” shouts Johnny. “Help!”

Johnny runs to Charlie’s aide, diving into the pool and dragging him out. Johnny lays Charlie onto the timber deck. Johnny checks Charlie's pulse by pressing his index finger into his neck. Nothing. Johnny begins to give Charlie CPR. Blood spills from Charlie’s head wound. Georgie licks the wound.

In between Johnny’s compressions of Charlie’s chest, Nicole comes running out into the backyard.

Nicole asks, “Oh no, what happened?”

Johnny responds, “What happened, I should be asking you that question!”

Nicole freezes like a deer caught in the headlights.

Johnny stops the compressions and gives Charlie two rescue breaths, mouth-to-mouth.
Anna runs outside to the harrowing scene and immediately takes control of the situation.

"Does he have a pulse?" Anna asks.

"No!" Johnny responds, continuing with the compressions.

Anna takes out her phone and calls triple zero. Emergency services answers the phone.

"What's your emergency?"
"My brother isn't breathing"
"What happened?"
"We found him face down in the pool."
"Does he have a pulse?"
"No."
"Has anyone started CPR?"
"Yes, my dad."
"Does he need any assistance with the CPR?"
"No. He knows first aide."
"An Ambulance is on the way"
"Please hurry!"
Anna hangs up.

Nicole stands frozen like a statue. Georgie licks Charlie's head wound.

Johnny says, "Nicole! Help stop the bleeding!"
Nicole pushes Georgie out of the way and presses a towel up against Charlie's head wound.

An ambulance with all the lights and sirens speeds down the street and pulls into their driveway. Two ambulance officers come quickly through the side fence with their equipment. They hurry around the back to the pool area where Johnny is administering CPR to Charlie.

The female officer says “We'll take it from here, sir. How long have you been administering CPR?”

Johnny says, “Five minutes or so.”

The ambulance officers turn their resuscitation machine on, and one officer places the shock nodes onto Charlie's chest.

The female officer says, “3…2…1…Clear!” and administers the electric shock.

The male ambulance officer checks Charlie's pulse and shakes his head from side to side.

The female officer says, “3...2...1…Clear!” and administers a second shock.

The male officer checks Charlie’s pulse again and shakes his head. The situation now hopeless, he says “I’m really sorry.”

Nicole backs slowly away. She puts her hand to her mouth, finding it difficult to breathe.

Johnny slumps to his knees and cries out.

Anna, tears streaming down her face, comforts Johnny by hugging him.

Chapter 3
Alice's Graveyard

It is half past midnight, and the Beast is parked at an abandoned area by a large watering hole. This is where Alice was baptized many moons ago.

Alice sits in the prime mover and watches the CCTV monitor, which links to the video feed inside the trailer. Justice's wild eyes glow amber within the darkness of the trailer. Alice remotely switches on the lights inside the trailer. Justice barks ferociously, angry that his mealtime has been disturbed. Justice, after all, enjoys dining in the darkness. The fur around his mouth is dark and blood stained.

The trailer lights reveal human remains scattered all over the trailer floor. Justice lies with his stomach on the floor, chewing on Matt’s calf. Matt's severed arms are still attached to the chains and are curing like fine meat. Blood drips down from the severed limbs.

Alice’s voice comes through the trailer speaker, “Morning, Justice. I think you have a bit more work to do here.”

Justice launches from his sitting position and leaps up at Matt’s severed arms. Justice rips and tears at the arms until he pulls them free of the restraints.

Alice, holding the two-way, says, “Good boy Justice!”

On the control panel Alice flicks through to different video feeds. The trailer floor is doused in blood and guts.

Alice continues, "But the floor is a mess Justice. And you know what that means. It's bath time for you and the Beast".

Justice looks up with trepidation. And when Justice is anxious, his bowels become loose. Justice squats on the haunches of his hind legs and releases his bowels on the trailer floor.

Justice looks up guiltily to the camera lens, as Alice says, "Justice, you dirty dog. Always at bath time…"

When he finishes laying cable Justice scoots his bum along the trailer floor.

"Do your anal glands need a squeeze, Justice?", Alice asks.

Justice barks his disapproval. The last person who tried to squeeze Justice's anal glands had their fingers bitten off.

Alice starts the engine. Alice puts the truck into reverse. The Beast reverses down the dirt embankment directly into the watering hole. The trailer tires roll into the water. Operating the control panel, Alice remotely lowers the tailgate. Justice moves swiftly to the front of the trailer.

The tailgate lowers down into the water. The water creeps along the trailer floor towards Justice, who anxiously moves around at the front of the trailer. He hates bath time. Justice whimpers and cowers as the water goes over the top of his paws. The truck reverses further and water continues to flow into the trailer.

Justice howls as he is fully immersed in the water. The water engulfs him up to his neck. Guts, bones, Matt's severed head and Justice's poo float around in the trailer. Justice swims around in the sullied water. The truck comes to a stop.

Alice puts the truck into first gear and drives forward. All the rubbish gets washed towards the back of the trailer. Matt's severed head is a souvenir that must be kept for Justice's master. Justice hurries over to Matt's head and bites hold of it by the ear. The Beast drives out of the watering hole and the trailer floor gets cleaned out. Everything but Matt's head which Justice holds by the ear.

Once on dry land Alice remotely closes the tailgate. Soaked in water, Justice has his usual post-bath meltdown. He sprints madly around the trailer and shakes the water from his fur. Then, Justice relaxes with his belly on the trailer floor after his post bath meltdown. Justice tears off Matt's ear from the head and chews it hungrily. Ears make for a tasty treat. But this is against his master's wishes.

Alice blows a whistle which elicits a high-pitched sound. Justice is getting a little too comfortable. The head is to be left alone.

Justice ignores Alice and stays laid out on his tummy, crunching on the ear cartilage of the head he holds between his paws. Alice blows the whistle again, only this time, more forcefully. It makes a deafening sound through the trailer speaker.

There is a pause as Justice contemplates his next move. Then, as if realizing his master has the upper hand Justice returns to his cage, leaving Matt's head, minus one ear, on the trailer floor. The cage door locks automatically behind him.

Alice smiles grimly. Another head for his trophy room.

Chapter 4
Black Days

Anna wakes to find Georgie licking her face. “Yuck… Georgie!” Anna says, pushing Georgie away.

Anna follows her usual morning routine. She gets up and gives Georgie lots of pats. Georgie loves the morning pats almost as much as he loves his treats. Georgie raises his front paws onto Anna’s ample chest to stretch and Anna tickles his tummy.

“Down Georgie” Anna says.

Georgie drops back down.

Anna goes into the kitchen with Georgie shadowing behind her.

Anna goes to the fridge to get Georgie’s breakfast meat log. There is a picture on the fridge from last Halloween of Anna and Charlie dressed up as ‘Carrie’ and ‘Freddy Krueger’, respectively. Charlie holds up the razor glove to Anna, who wears a red-stained dress and red body paint. Anna recalls her initial reluctance to pose with Charlie. But then Charlie had made it fun. Her eyes well up with tears. She cannot believe Charlie is gone. Even though they fought a lot, he was her kid brother. And life will never be the same.

As if feeling Anna’s anxiety, Georgie slumps sadly on the floor.

Anna fills Georgie's food and water bowl. Georgie's tail wags in anticipation. Once Anna steps away, Georgie hungrily devours his food. Like clockwork Georgie finishes the meal and runs for Charlie's room to wake the boy. Nicole sits on Charlie's bed, weeping as she goes through his photo album. She has been crying most of the night.

Georgie jumps on the bed and licks Nicole's arm to comfort her. Georgie's licking drives her mad. Nicole pushes Georgie away.

Nicole says, "Stop it, Georgie! Bad dog!"

Anna comes to the doorway of Charlie's bedroom.

Anna says, "Georgie, outside!"

Georgie jumps down from the bed and runs outside.

An emotional Nicole says, “Anna, you should get ready for school”.

“What? I’m not going to school today” Anna replies.

“We have to organize Charlie’s funeral. It would be better if you were not here.”

“I can help.”

Nicole says, “You can’t! You never help with anything! You’re a loser like your mum!”

“You bitch!”

Hearing the commotion, an exhausted Johnny comes down the hallway.

“What’s going on here?” Johnny asks.

“I can’t live here with her anymore! I’m going to live with my real mum!” Anna shouts.

“That’s fine with me! Go live with your junkie mum! You deserve each other!” Nicole shouts, clearly losing her nerve.

“It would be easier if she isn’t here, Johnny!” Nicole screams. “She goes to school today.”

“It’s your fault that Charlie is dead! You left the pool gate open!” Anna says.

Nicole visibly distressed, her body shaking, shouts “You miserable fucking cunt!”

Johnny firmly says, "Stop it! Both of you!"

Johnny walks over to Nicole and hugs her.

"Tell her, Johnny" Nicole says, between sobs.

Johnny says, "Anna. We're planning Charlie's funeral today. You better go to school to keep the peace."

"That's right! Take her side like you always do!" Anna shouts. Anna storms up the stairs and into her bedroom, slamming the door shut behind her.

Officer Robert Bates, 'Rob' to his mates, is a 45-year-old police officer who wears his uniform with pride. It is ironed with sharp corners. It hangs well on his slim figure and complements his neatly trimmed moustache and sophisticated glasses. Rob has been a policeman for all his adult life. He never desired to do anything else. He loves being a Highway Patrolman. There is nobody watching over his shoulder, and he has the freedom to do his job how he wants to do it. When he was offered a promotion to be Senior Constable in Kruger, he knocked it back. Why would he want to be tied down in 'Deadsville' Kruger where nothing exciting ever happens? Despite his quiet, relaxed demeanor, there is a dark cloud that hovers over Rob. Something from his past that he cannot seem to shake off.

Officer Rob Bates drives a v8 patrol car. It is an ideal vehicle for a fast car chase on the open highway. Rob's patrol car approaches Matt's burnt-out Ute and Rob pulls over adjacent to it.

He gets out and scans the crime scene. Rob shines his torch over the smoldering remains of Matt's Ute. The charcoal corpse of Joe has been reduced to ashes. Rob shines his torch on a trail of petrol that leads from the wreckage to a cigarette butt in the gravel. Rob turns his attention to truck tire skid marks on the highway. But the truck is long gone by now, so Rob returns to his police car. Inside the patrol car, Rob takes out his mobile phone to call an old friend.

At Kruger Scrap Metal Recycling Yard, a giant crane with a steel mechanical claw, crawls over a mass of metal. The claw grabs hold of a massive clump of metal, picks it up and dumps it on top of a conveyor that feeds into a metal shredding machine.

Inside the main office is a fat man named Slim. Loud sexual moaning sounds come from Slim's computer. Slim is eating fried chicken and watching videos from his favorite porn site, 'Busty Babes Hunter'. The phone rings. Slim's wife sits in the adjacent office. She answers the phone. "Scrap Metal Recycling, Maryanne speaking…"

Pause.

Maryanne continues, "Ok, I'll just put you through to him…"

She passes the call into Slim's office. The phone rings for what seems like an eternity. Slim is glued to the computer screen, watching a busty blonde bimbo moaning as she is being shagged in a shower by a man with a long appendage.

"Pick up the phone you pig" Maryanne calls out.

Slim turns down the volume on his computer. He checks the caller ID and answers, "I'm busy! What is it?"

Rob, sitting in his patrol car, says, "Slim, I've got another burnt-out wreck for you."

"Where is it?"

"Dead Valley Highway."

"It's gonna cost ya double this time!"

"OK, Slim. Just take care of it".

"Send me location."

Slim hangs up the phone and turns the volume back up on the computer. The big breasted blonde babe is screaming with pleasure as the 'Busty

Babes Hunter' penetrates her from behind. Her big tits rub up and down against the shower screen almost busting through the glass.

"Oh yeah, baby" Slim says, his eyes glued to the screen.

A white Cross signifying the crucifixion of Christ looms large over a Catholic School in suburbia. In the school courtyard, Anna sits with her portly friend Melissa eating a sandwich. Melissa is enjoying all the trappings – a hamburger and hot chips drenched in sauce, washing it all down with a chocolate shake. Melissa does most of the talking whilst Anna is distracted by this morning's conflict with her stepmother.

Anna sits in a school skirt with her legs apart and stretched out, unaware her knickers are on full display to a group of horny teenage schoolboys across the schoolyard. The schoolboys are being crass and full of bravado, joking and giving each other high fives at what they would do to the sweet

Anna. They are full of machismo within the safety of their clique. One disgusting boy has his phone out and is filming Anna from a distance, trying to zoom in on her knickers.

A small group of girls watches the boys ogling and being crass towards Anna. They are led by another pretty girl, Karen, who is clearly agitated by the attention Anna is receiving from the group of boys.

"She's such a slut! Look at her, displaying her filthy gash for all the boys to gawk at!" Karen says to the group.

They nod and voice their agreement. Anna is oblivious to the kerfuffle.

Karen shouts out to Anna from across the schoolyard, "Hey, you dumb slut! Why don't you put an 'open for business' sign on your knickers?"

Anna looks up and, seeing all the attention on her, quickly pulls her skirt down and crosses her legs.

"Those boys are so feral," Melissa says to Anna. "Especially Glen. I bet he chokes the chicken over you every night."

With her right-hand Melissa acts out a man masturbating, then mocks Glen's voice, saying "Oh Anna. Oh Anna. I wanna be your one and only…"

"Eeeww, Melissa, that's so disgusting!" Anna replies.

Melissa laughs. The school bell sounds, signaling the end of lunch. Anna and Melissa pack their lunch bags to return to the classroom.

"I'll see you later Mel," Anna says.

“Righto,” replies Melissa, polishing off the remains of her shake.

Anna goes to the bathroom. She does not realize that Karen and three from her clique are tailing her. There are five stalls inside the bathroom. Anna enters the first stall to find the toilet water soaked with period blood. Someone has not had the decency to flush it away.

“Oh gross!” Anna says in disgust.

She enters the next stall, which is clean enough, and places toilet paper on the toilet seat. As she sits down, Karen and her friends enter the bathroom. Karen bangs heavily on Anna’s stall door.

“This one’s taken,” Anna says.

Karen stands on a toilet seat in the adjacent stall and looks over into Anna’s stall.

Karen, clearly agitated, says, “Yeah, we know. It’s the filthy slut who put on quite a show at lunchtime.”

The other girls snicker and laugh.

Anna replies, “I didn’t know they were gawking at me.”

Karen says, “We’ve got something for you. Come out or we’ll bash the door in!”

Anna says, “Fuck off Karen!”

Karen kicks the door in, grabs Anna and drags her out of the stall.

“Everyone takes pity on you. Just because your junkie mum abandoned you. Well, the apple doesn't fall far from the tree," Karen says.

"Leave me alone", Anna says.

"Well, 'Boo Hoo'! We girls know what game you're playing at. You didn't get enough attention from Mummy and Daddy, so now you want it from all the boys at school."

"Shut up!" Anna shouts.

The other girls giggle. Anna is burning with anger at Karen's insults and bullying. Anna wrestles against Karen's grip on her.

"Grab her!" Karen orders. Karen's friends grab Anna by either arm.

"Drag her in there!" Karen barks, pointing to the stall with the bloodied toilet water.

With Karen pulling her hair and two other girls dragging her by the arms, Anna is forced into the stall. Karen trips Anna to the ground. The girls force Anna's head towards the toilet bowl. Anna fights back with all her strength, but it is a losing battle.

"You've had this coming to you bitch! Like your brother!" Karen shouts.

"No! No! No!" shouts Anna as her head is pushed down into the toilet bowl.

The blood-soaked water washes over Anna's face and, to her disgust, she inhales a mouthful. All of Karen's past insults and bullying come to the surface as Anna swallows the sullied water. It is as though the bottle has been shaken one too many times and now it has been uncorked. Anna is filled with blood curdling anger and a fiery, tormented bitch is unleashed. Anna bites down hard on one girl's hand. The girl screams out in pain and releases her grip on Anna.

Anna twists around and grabs Karen by the throat. Anna slams Karen's face into the porcelain toilet bowl. There is a loud bone shattering sound as Karen's cheekbone shatters. A large gash opens on her face.

"Aagh!" Karen screams out as the deep gash bleeds profusely. She rolls around in agony grabbing her face. Anna attempts to flee the bathroom in a hurry. As she is fleeing, the math teacher, Mrs. Avery, comes into the bathroom, blocking Anna's exit.

"Why are all you girls screaming?" Mrs. Avery asks.

"Anna attacked Karen!" Karen's clique shouts.

"They came at me first!" Anna says defiantly.

"We did not!" the girls' shout. "Anna's a psycho! Look at what she did to Karen's face."

"And she bit my hand!" one girl says, holding up her gnawed hand.

Mrs. Avery kneels next to Karen and sees all the blood coming from Karen's facial wound.

"Show me," Mrs. Avery says to Karen.

Karen takes her hand away from her face.

"Oh dear!" Mrs. Avery says.

She turns to face Anna and says, "What have you done Anna?"

Anna, realizing the gravity of the incident and being outnumbered by Karen's friends, runs away from the scene. She only wants to get her bag and run home. As she runs back to the locker room, a strong male arm grabs her on the shoulder.

"Where are you off to?" the school Principal asks.

"They attacked me! I was defending myself," Anna says.

"We'll see about that," the principal says. "Come to my office."

There is quite a commotion in the bathroom as more people come to see what has transpired. Mrs. Avery is holding wet paper towels against Karen's face to stop the bleeding. Young girls try to video Karen and get a quality picture of Karen's facial wound for social media.

Later, Anna sits in the principal's office with her dad Johnny beside her. The principal stands opposite them on the other side of the desk. The authoritarian principal shouts and gesticulates his disgust at Anna's actions. Anna answers back but Johnny grabs her by the wrist and signals her to be quiet. Anna slumps into her chair, discouraged that her own father is not supporting her. She quietly succumbs to her fate, knowing that she is not going to get a fair trial, that school suspension or expulsion is imminent, but not really caring either way. The principal points to the door and shouts, "OUT! We don't want girls like you in our school!"

Later that night, there is a full moon in the night sky. Johnny and Nicole are sleeping in the upstairs bedroom.

Anna, wearing a tight-fitting t-shirt over her large breasts and skinny cutoff pants which accentuate her long legs, packs a bag with some belongings. For Anna, it's time to escape this hellhole. Georgie is slumped on the bed, watching sadly on, knowing that something is not right with the girl. Anna is Georgie's closest friend. Now the girl is leaving. Georgie whines.
"Quiet Georgie" Anna says, not wanting Johnny or Nicole to awake.
Anna cannot stay. She has had enough of her stepmother and the abuse she is copping at school. She is sick to death of being treated like an expendable piece of furniture. It is time to take off. Besides, Anna is desperate to see her mother in Kruger.
Georgie shadows Anna down the stairs and into the living room. Anna takes the keys for her dad's Volvo prime mover truck. Anna could have taken the keys for Nicole's Mini but she would surely call the police on her. Besides, Anna likes the truck. She feels powerful driving it, sitting up high and looking over the other traffic. She has driven the truck before with her father riding shotgun. The truck has an automatic transmission and sophisticated driver features that make it easy to drive for just about anyone. 'We're one generation away from driverless trucks', her father would often say.

Anna says her last goodbyes to Georgie. She gives Georgie a big hug and kisses him on top of the head. Georgie rolls onto his back and Anna pats him on the belly one last time.

"Shameless", Anna says affectionately.

Anna leaves the house and shuts the door. Anna unlocks the prime mover and climbs up the stairs into the cab of the truck. She puts her backpack on the passenger seat and turns on the ignition. The engine turns over and the lights come on. Anna adjusts the seat position. A red warning light shows on the front dash. 'ADBLUE CRITICALLY LOW'. Anna knows that AdBlue helps decrease the emissions from the truck but figures it should run fine without it.

She reverses the truck out onto the street. Anna drives the truck through the dimly lit suburban streets. Luckily, Johnny has left the truck with a full tank of fuel, so Anna will not need to stop for a while. She has a long trip ahead and she wants to keep moving. The further she can get away from this shit town, the better. Anna finds a certain comfort in driving the prime mover at night. But that is soon brought to a crumbling halt.

Anna takes a turnoff for the on ramp that leads onto the highway. Anna gets onto the on-ramp and speeds up to merge. A B-Double truck lit up like a Christmas tree drives along the one lane highway. With Anna about to merge, the truck driver blows the air horn and cuts Anna off.

"Oh shit! Just what I needed!" Anna says.

Anna presses the foot brake and lets the B-Double truck pass in front of her. He's in a great big rush so Anna lets him pass in front.

Suddenly, an alarm goes off and a red warning light flashes on the front dash, which reads 'NO ADBLUE - TURN ENGINE OFF'. The truck loses power and Anna is forced to pull the truck off the road and onto the shoulder of the highway. The truck stalls inches from a streetlight post.

Anna tries to restart the truck without success.

"Aagh!" Anna shouts.

What else could go wrong today, Anna thinks to herself. How is she going to get to her mother's place in Kruger without a car? She considers calling her dad, but she cannot bare to face him now. Not after all that has been said. Also, he is going to be really pissed when he finds out she took off in his prized truck and it broke down.

Anna grabs her bag and locks up the truck. She leaves the key on the front driver-side tire. Desperate times call for desperate measures. Anna stands underneath the streetlight and sticks her thumb out, hoping to hitch a ride. Looking as hot as she does, it does not take long for someone to stop for her.

A white combi van covered with Christian indoctrination like 'Jesus is Risen' and 'God Forgives' pulls over on the shoulder of the highway. Anna approaches the passenger side window. Danny, a 55-year-old preacher, drives the combi. He is an immaculately kept man with tidy black hair and glasses.

"Where are you going darling?" Danny asks.

"To see my mum in Kruger"

"Today's your lucky day. Jump in."

"Thank you".

Anna jumps in the back of the combi. Anna stretches out on the seat, her long legs extending along the seat.

Danny says, "That seat is surprisingly comfortable. Why don't you get some rest darling?"

"Thank you" Anna responds, closing her eyes.

Danny perves on Anna's legs through the rearview mirror.

Back in suburbia, Nicole wakes Johnny.

"What is it?" Johnny asks.

"Your precious daughter has taken off in your truck".

"What?" Johnny says.

"She's taken some of her belongings too".

"Oh shit!" Johnny says, getting up.

Johnny attempts to call Anna. There is no answer from Anna's end and the phone rings out.

Johnny says, "Hang on. I should be able to track her mobile."

Johnny opens the Life 360 app on his phone. A GPS tracker comes up on Johnny's phone showing the location of Anna's phone.

"Where is she?" Nicole asks.

"On the highway to Kruger."

"To her mums'?"

"Yeah. Let's go get her!"

"Is that the best thing to do Johnny? Maybe we should let her go. She'll come back. She always does."

“No darling. I couldn’t buy any AdBlue! And the truck cannot run without it! It will simply stop!”

Johnny grabs the keys for Nicole’s Mini car from the kitchen bench.

“Are you coming?” Johnny asks.

“Ok. Since you’re taking my car.”

Georgie barks his enthusiasm to go along with them.

“You can come too, Georgie” Johnny says.

Johnny moves with great urgency to the garage. Georgie follows him closely with Nicole reluctantly in tow. Nicole gets in the passenger seat and Georgie in the back of the Mini.

Johnny reverses the Mini out of the garage and accelerates down the street at speed.

CHAPTER 5
Alice

Alice's truck, the 'BEAST', is parked at the back of Roxy's Roadhouse, the only refueling station on Dead Valley Highway. Roxy's is Alice's most frequented hunting spot. Customers are few and far between. Just how Alice likes it.

Inside the Beast, Alice sharpens his hunting knife on a steel block. The blade makes a metallic, high-pitched sound as it sharpens on the steel block. Alice takes great pride in the sharpening of the knife. He looks forward to using the newly sharpened blade. Killing the boys has given Alice an appetite for more blood.

Alice looks over to the human foot bone in the glass box. This memento is to remind Alice of the day he vowed never again to be a victim. The day that set him on his path to become the Highway Hunter. The memories from that day consume him.

It was a beautiful summer's day in the leafy suburb of Kruger, with the birds chirping and the trees lush and green. In the center of town, a striking white cathedral was distinguishable by the extraordinary white cross on the roof.

Young choirboys were singing the final hymn, marking the end of the Sunday service. The parishioners began to exit the cathedral. In the basement, two altar boys dressed in white Alb robes were up to no good.

Alice, eyes already dark at just 9 years old, carried the sacramental wine ciborium. Bobby, 8, was a fat boy with a stutter who wore nerdy bottle cap glasses. Bobby carried the Eucharistic bread monstrance and holy cup to the piscina. The monstrance was metallic with a sharp metal cross on top.

Alice challenged Bobby, "Bobby, let's finish the bread and wine."

Bobby said, "N-n-no way, Alice. Fa-fa-father Bell will go nuts."

Alice belittled Bobby, saying, "What are you scared of Blubbering Bobby? That he'll play with your doodle?"

“I wo-wo-won’t ever let him touch me again! Ne-ne-never!”

“What are you scared of then?”

“I-I-I’m not scared, Alice.”

“Prove it!”

“O-o-kay.”

Alice said, “Race ya. Loser has to help Bell pack up.”

Unbeknown to the boys, the imposing figure of Father Bell wearing a white cassock robe and holding a long metal crosier stood in the doorway, watching the boys. Alice raised the ciborium and sculled the wine. Bobby grabbed a handful of holy bread and shoved it into his mouth. But he had difficulty swallowing the dry bread. He reached for the ciborium in Alice's hands and dropped the holy cup and Eucharistic bread all over the floor. The ciborium fell onto the carpet and stained it with red, consecrated wine.

Father Bell, 60 years old, stamped his crosier heavily onto the floor, making a loud thumping sound.

“Dear Lord, what is going on here?” Bell shouted. “You are disgraceful, naughty little boys!”

Father Bell charged at the boys, carrying the crosier. Alice ran to the other side of the room, as Bobby stood frozen still. Father Bell grabbed Bobby by the arm. Bobby dropped the monstrance. Father Bell smacked Bobby across the back of the head. Bobby started to cry.

Bobby pleads, “S-s-sorry Father.”

"Stop blubbering, you stupid fat boy. You have disgraced our Savior. You must pay the consequences!"

"T-t-ten Hail Mary's?"

"Here is your forgiveness Blubber Boy."

Father Bell put down the crosier and lifted his robe, exposing himself to the boy.

"N-n-no F-F-Father! NO!"

Alice came up behind and picked up the crosier. He slammed the crosier down on Father Bell's head with a heavy blow. It knocked Bell to his knees. Father Bell reached for his head as blood spilt out of the wound. To Bell's dismay his hand came away bloodied.

Alice swung the Crosier down on Father Bell's head again. More blood came out, spilling onto the carpet. Alice dropped the crosier as blood poured from Bell's head. Bell took an emergency whistle from his pocket and blew heavily to elicit a deafening, high-pitched sound.

Bell shouted out with sinister anger, "Release the hounds!"

Inside a dark room there were two terrifying, wild American pit bulls in a cage. They bared their rabid teeth, frothing at the mouth with ferocious fits of hunger. Their amber eyes shone into the pitch-black room. The dogs were eager to kill. A little creepy old man with a big nose wearing a flowing black robe stood at the top of a staircase in the room. He pressed a button on a remote control. The cage door that secured the pit bulls opened wide. The wild dogs raced out of the cage and out of the room. The pit bulls barked with vicious intent. In the basement Bobby shouted to Alice, "R-r-run Alice!! R-r-run!"

Alice ran outside the church and onto the grass. He ran for the fence as he heard the wild pit bulls growling and hunting for his blood. The pit bulls grunted and growled as they launched into the yard baying for Alice's blood. Alice took a spill near the back gate as the hungry dogs closed in on him. To his dismay, the back gate was padlocked. Alice turned around. The wild dogs were within striking distance.

Alice climbed the six-foot high wooden fence, which had barbed wire along the top. Sweat ran down Alice's brow. The grunts and the heavy breathing of the killer dogs were closing in on him. Alice reached up and grabbed the barbed wire, which cut his hands and drew blood. He raised himself up, but his shirt got tangled in the barbed wire and he could not free himself. The wild dogs jumped for his foot. One of the dogs clenched his jaws onto Alice's left foot.

Alice screamed out in agony, "Aagh!"

The fierce animal ripped through Alice's left shoe, tearing into the flesh in his foot. Blood poured out, turning the white sneaker blood red. The wild dog tore the sole off Alice's sneaker, allowing him to break free, untangle himself from the barbed wire and pull himself over the fence to safety. Once he was on the safe side of the fence, he looked down at his mangled foot. The wild pit bulls barked viciously from the other side of the fence. Alice rolled around crying in agony.

Alice brings his focus back to the present, to the foot bone in the glass box, and to the sharpening of the knife on the steel block. The high-pitched metallic sound of the sharpening knife soothes Alice and puts him in a hypnotic trance. The hunger to kill eats at him. The time will come soon enough to use the blade. The sooner, the better, he thinks.

Preacher Danny's combi turns into Roxy's Roadhouse.

"Wakey-wake, sleepy head", Danny says.

Anna opens her eyes.

"We've reached a pit stop", Danny says.

Anna yawns and stretches out her limbs.

Danny parks next to a fuel bowser and gets out of the combi. He takes the pump from the bowser and pumps petrol into the combi. Alice watches from the prime mover of his Beast.

Anna gets out of the combi to stretch her limbs. Her skinny cut-off pants and tight t-shirt accentuate her considerable assets. She is a vision of beauty the likes of which Alice sees very rarely. Her womanly figure and tender young flesh fill Alice with desire and hunger. She would be a perfect addition to his mantelpiece.

Anna walks to the back of the Roadhouse following a sign for the bathroom. Alice's gaze stalks her. He is aroused by the girl, but he feels compelled to find out more about her. What is she doing with that old preacher? Is she in trouble?

Anna enters the bathroom with caution. The door creaks open. The bathroom is dark and dingy with profuse graffiti covering the walls. The floor is filthy. She sees a used condom on the floor.

"Oh my. Disgusting", Anna says.

She enters a stall and locks the door. Anna wipes down the seat with toilet paper. She places paper down to cover the seat and sits down.

The bathroom door creaks open. Big black boots shuffle into the bathroom. Anna sits with bated breath. The big black boots shuffle towards her toilet stall. A strong hand knocks on Anna's toilet door. For Anna it is a feeling of de ja vu. Could it be that Karen's clique have come after her? Anna looks underneath the toilet stall. Rugged, black boots belonging to a very big man stand outside her toilet.

Anna utters, "This one's taken."

There is no reply. The black boots stay put, not moving an inch.

Anna closes her eyes and takes some deep breaths. After a pause, she opens her eyes, pulls up her knickers and flushes the toilet. Anna unlocks the door and swings it wide open. Her eyes scan the room. The bathroom is empty.

Anna exits the bathroom. Outside the bathroom, Anna stands still, staring suspiciously towards the black truck parked at the back of Roxy's. Anna feels a sense of unease that a dark presence lurks within the truck.

Alice ogles Anna from the prime mover. This chance encounter with her has set off his predatory instincts. He must have her. And killing the preacher will be a nice little bonus. Alice will take great pleasure in gutting him with his newly sharpened knife.

Danny returns to the combi with two drinks. Alice starts the engine of the Beast. The anticipation of a highway hunt has Alice brimming with excitement. The combi heads back onto the highway. Alice puts the Beast into gear and follows them.

Johnny accelerates the Mini along the highway whilst Nicole rides shotgun. Georgie has his head out the window in the back, feeling the wind blowing in his face. Johnny follows the GPS on his mobile phone which is tracking Anna's phone. The phone is set up in a holder on the front windscreen of the car. Georgie stands at attention on the center console and barks at something up ahead. Johnny's prime mover truck is parked where Anna left it under a streetlight on the shoulder of the highway.

"She didn't get very far…" Nicole says.

"It must've run empty of AdBlue" Johnny replies.

Johnny drives onto the gravel and parks in front of the prime mover. Johnny rushes over and unlocks the cab with his spare key. There is no sign of Anna or her belongings inside the driver cab. Johnny returns to the Mini.

"Where is she?" Nicole asks.

Johnny, looking at the GPS tracker, says, "She must've hitched a ride. She's a couple hundred clicks ahead of us."

"Can you drive the truck and I'll take the Mini back home?"

"No. The truck will not run without AdBlue."

Johnny accelerates the Mini back onto the highway, following the mobile app which is tracking Anna's mobile location.

Down the highway from Roxy's Roadhouse, Danny's combi begins having trouble. The temperature gauge is on high, and the engine starts to splutter.

"What's the matter?" Anna asks.

Danny says, "The engine is overheating."

Anna responds, "Great! It must be my lucky day."

Steam starts to dissipate from under the bonnet. A red radiator light flashes on the front dash and a warning alarm sounds off. The engine snuffs off and on, causing the combi to stutter. But a much bigger problem is about to present itself.

The Beast comes roaring up behind them at full tilt. Smoke, soot and flames flare out of the Beast's twin exhaust pipes. Anna looks behind as Alice's truck accelerates to within inches of the combi. The Beast's air horn rings in the ears of Anna and Danny. The Beast is all intimidation and menace.

Anna says, "Jesus Christ!"

"Don't use the Lord's name in vain!" Danny says.

Anna slumps further back into her seat. The truck's loud, overbearing exhaust brakes come on to back the Beast off. Danny opens the driver side window, sticks his arm out and waves Alice on.

Alice accelerates alongside the combi and boxes it in tightly. Alice turns on the hazard lights and waves at the preacher to pullover.

Danny says, "We should pull over."

Anna shouts, "That's a really bad idea!"

The combi loses engine power as more smoke comes from the engine. Danny rolls the combi off the road and onto the gravel. He slows down.

Danny says, "Have some faith." But Anna is not so naïve to believe that God will help them.

Anna begs, "Please, I've got a bad feeling about this."

Danny says, "It's in God's hands now."

"D'ya think God is gonna help us now?"

Danny brings the combi to a stop.

There is a loud engine roar as the Beast slows rapidly down. Alice pulls the truck over in front of the combi.

Inside the combi, Anna is anxious whilst Danny remains optimistic. Danny says, "Everything will be fine. Just wait here."

Anna says, "Don't worry, I have no intention of following you."

CHAPTER 6
Justice

Alice's big black boots step down from the truck. He shuffles along the gravel to the combi. Danny waits to confront him for his reckless driving.

Danny says, "What's with the tailgating and blowing the horn?"

"Sorry mate. Did I scare you?"

"You startled the girl."

Alice looks with piercing eyes towards Anna. He restrains himself as the young teen has him hot under the collar. He desperately wants a piece of that ass, but he must play nice, keeping his ultimate plans close to his chest.

"I'm sorry."

Alice extends out his hand, then continues, "the name's Alice".

"Danny." They shake hands. "That's a firm grip you have Alice."

Alice says, "I used to work in the abattoir carving up pig and cow carcasses. But the job became too hard on account of my wooden leg."

Alice lifts the left pant up. Below his knee stump Alice has an artificial leg. He knocks on the wooden leg.

Danny says, "I bet that makes for a good party trick…"

Alice smiles, saying "Well, Danny boy, best we check your engine. I'm on a deadline to deliver this load of frozen meat to Kruger tonight."

Danny flips up the bonnet and a plume of smoke rises into the sky. Alice looks underneath the chassis and sees coolant leaking onto the ground.

Alice says, "Fuck me dead, buddy! That doesn't look too good. Check the radiator."

Danny grabs the hot radiator cap and turns it. Smoke blows the cap off, burning his hand. Danny winces in pain. He keels over, holding his scorched hand. With Danny being preoccupied with his burnt hand, Alice seizes his opportunity. Alice pulls the hunting knife out from the scabbard of his belt.

Alice raises his hunting knife, saying, "Night-night, Preacher."

Alice thrusts the knife into Danny's back. The preacher cries out and his eyes go wide with shock. Alice withdraws the blade and Danny falls to the ground, gravely injured.

Anna screams, "Nooo!"

Alice shuffles towards Anna, who jumps into the driver seat of the combi. A panicked Anna hurriedly turns the key in the ignition. The combi does not start. Alice rushes to the driver side door. Anna locks the door. Alice calmly knocks on the window with the butt of the knife and says, "Open the door please."

Anna turns the ignition again. This time the engine starts up. Anna puts the combi into gear.

Alice shouts, "I said pleeeease!" and smashes the driver side window with the butt of his knife. The glass falls inwards, all over Anna.

"Aagh!", she screams, as the glass shards scratch lacerations in her arms and face. The combi stalls.

Alice reaches in through the broken window, unlocks the door and opens it. Alice drags Anna out by the hair.

Anna screams for help.

Alice says, "Nobody will hear you scream out here."

Anna shouts, “Fuck off!”

Alice slams Anna into the combi, seemingly knocking her out. Alice drags Anna along the gravel to the back of the truck.

Operating the hand controls at the rear of the truck, he lowers the tailgate down to the ground. A pair of deadly canine eyes glow amber in the darkness of the trailer. Justice is aroused by Anna’s scent and barks viciously, baring his frothing teeth. Justice is a hungry, rabid beast and the girl would make for a tasty treat.

Alice marches onto the tailgate and tosses Anna’s body on the floor of the trailer. Justice slams against the cage walls, desperate to taste Anna. With her back to Alice, Anna opens her eyes.

Alice says, “Justice! You can lay down the law after I’m finished with her. But I'll have my fun first!”

The combi engine starts up. A bloodied and mortally wounded Danny attempts to drive away. But in his delirious state, the preacher loses control of the combi, drives into a ditch and crashes into a lone tree.

Alice charges towards the combi and rips the driver side door out. Danny is bleeding profusely in the driver seat. Alice drags Danny out by his collar.

Alice says, “You almost hit me preacher.”

Alice drags Danny along the gravel to the back of the truck. He will have his fun with them both. But Anna has gone.

"No!" he shouts.

Alice shines a torch inside the trailer. Only Justice is inside.

Alice scans the surrounding area for Anna using the torch. There are many bushes, shrubs and crevices nearby where Anna could be hiding.

Alice calls to his dog, "It's your turn to shine Justice!"

He takes out a remote control and presses a button on it. The steel cage door slides upwards. Alice takes the whistle out from his pocket and blows it, eliciting a high-pitched sound. The dog runs out of the cage and launches off the back of the trailer. The dog hunts for Anna in the surrounding area. Justice picks up Anna's scent and closes in on her location.

Anna shuffles on her backside into some bushes, watching with bated breath. She keeps her head down. Justice sniffs along Anna's trail towards the bushes.

Anna takes a deep breath and crawls behind a nearby rock to avoid Justice. But Justice is not the only predator around. A poisonous brown snake is nearby. Anna stops in her tracks as the brown snake slithers towards her Anna sits dead still. The brown snake readies to launch at her.

Justice appears out of the darkness and launches at the snake, grabbing it below the head and crushing it in his jaws. Justice shakes the snake vigorously. Anna gets onto her hands and knees and crawls into a nearby clearing. Justice decapitates the snake, but the tail of the snake continues to wriggle in his jaws.

Meanwhile on the highway, car headlights approach Alice's Beast from a kilometer away. Alice does not want to be disturbed. He drags Danny around to the side of the trailer not facing the highway.

A red v8 car drives past at high speed without stopping.

But Alice is losing patience. With a blow of the whistle, Alice calls his dog to return.

He shouts, “C'mon Justice!”

Justice, holding the headless snake in his jaws, runs back to the truck. Snakes make for a good entrée, but the main meal will have to wait.

“You captured the wrong snake boy,” Alice says.

Justice jumps into the trailer and returns to his cage. The gate to the cage shuts automatically behind him.

Alice calls out into the darkness, “You can't hide forever out there! Eventually you'll have to come out and we'll be waiting for you.”

CHAPTER 7
Hunted Down

Johnny accelerates the Mini at top speed.

"Anna is close!" Johnny says, looking at mobile GPS tracker.

"Maybe she lost her mobile" Nicole says.

"Shit! Shit!", Johnny says, stopping the car.

Aroused by something in the darkness, Georgie stands at attention on the center console and barks loudly into the front windscreen.

Johnny looks down at Georgie, "What's the matter buddy?"

Georgie's gaze is deadlocked on the road ahead, his tail points up into the air and the hairs along the spine of his back stand on end.

Johnny gets out of the car and looks down the highway. Suddenly, out of the blackness a visibly distressed girl runs down the highway waving her arms in the air, terrified.

Johnny says, "What in God's name?"

As the figure gets closer, it becomes clearer who it is.

"It's Anna!" Johnny exclaims, rushing towards her.

Georgie rushes passed Johnny. Anna collapses onto the middle of the highway and Georgie stands guard over her, licking her face.

Johnny quickly comes to her aid. Anna's clothes are torn, and she is covered in blood and dirt. Johnny checks her vital signs. Her heart is pumping hard.

"You're ok darling", he says.

Georgie, now standing at attention in the middle of the highway, resumes his barking into the darkness at the road ahead. Georgie's protective instincts are aroused, and he barks with piercing aggression into the darkness. Something has him spooked. Suddenly, bright headlights shine on them from a hundred meters away.

Alice sits in the Beast, with the engine idling, watching them. Alice revs the engine. Danny, barely alive, is chained to the front bulbar with his arms outstretched in a crucifix position. Alice moves the gear stick into a low gear and slowly accelerates towards them.

“Holy Mary Mother of God!” Johnny exclaims.

Johnny picks Anna up and carries her in front with his arms outstretched. He runs as fast as he can back to the Mini. The Beast stalks slowly towards them. Georgie stands his ground in the middle of the highway and barks fiercely at the approaching Beast. Alice shifts the stick up a gear and accelerates.

“Oh Fuck!” Nicole exclaims. She accelerates the Mini towards Johnny.

Alice’s Beast closes in on the barking Georgie. Stupid dog, Alice thinks. Continues to bark madly even though he’s about to be mashed into minced meat. But at the last second, Georgie jumps out of the path of the oncoming truck. Alice shifts the stick up a gear and accelerates harder.

The Mini stops in front of Johnny. Johnny lays Anna down on the backseat and gets swiftly into the passenger side of the Mini. The Beast accelerates hard at them, and Alice blares the air horn.

Nicole accelerates and steers the Mini away from the oncoming truck, avoiding impact and total obliteration. Alice is furious at missing them. Alice drives the Beast off the road and does a big looping U-turn in the gravel. Nicole accelerates the Mini.

“Hold up!” Johnny shouts.

“What?” Nicole replies.

"Stop for Georgie!"

Nicole pulls over. Johnny opens the passenger side door. Georgie runs in from the darkness and jumps into the passenger side of the Mini.

"I'll drive!" Johnny says.

Nicole and Johnny switch seats.

Johnny accelerates the Mini down the highway away from the Beast.

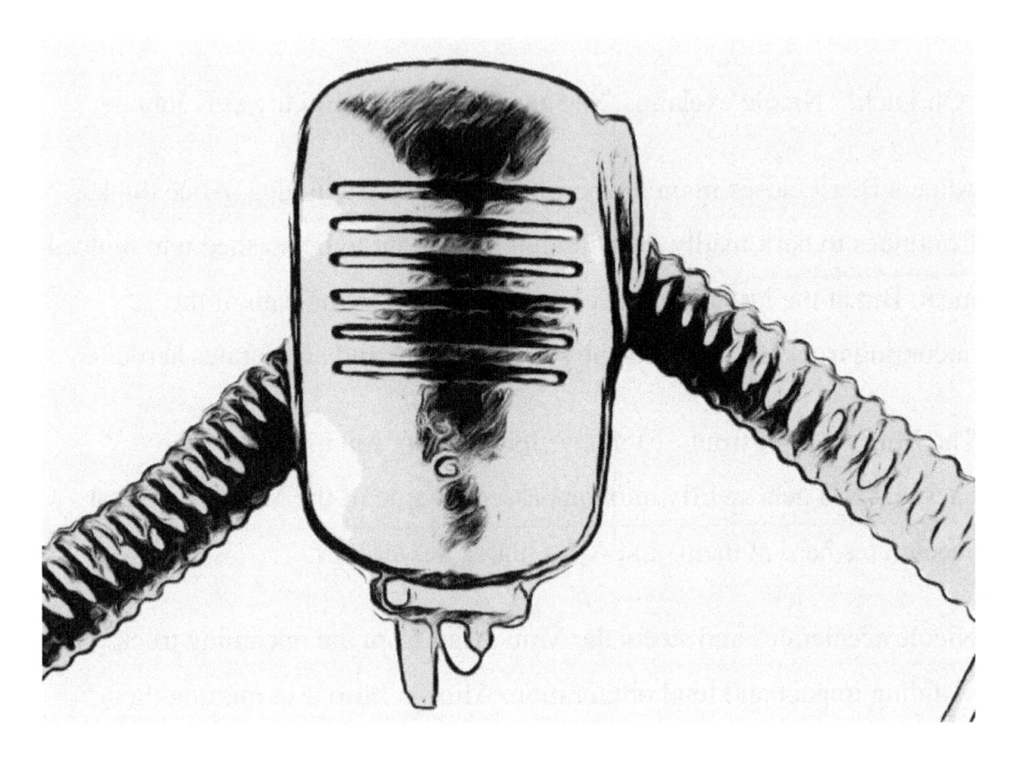

Loud static noise on the Mini radio. A deep, dark voice whispers, "Do you have something that belongs to me? You thief…"

Johnny flicks radio channels, but Alice controls the radio signal. Alice's crazed laugh comes through the radio.

“MWAH HA HA…”

Anna wakes up, incoherent and disorientated.

“AAGH!” Anna screams.

“You’re ok, darling. Its’ alright!”, Johnny says.

“You came for me”, Anna says. “Thank you”

Johnny says, “You are safe, darling daughter.”

A furious Alice drives the Beast back onto the highway towards the Mini. Looking in the rearview mirror, Nicole says, “He’s coming back around. There’s a man chained to the bulbar…”

“That’s the preacher!” Anna exclaims.

Johnny says, “Let’s get the hell outta here!” and puts his foot down on the accelerator.

Alice says, “You have nowhere to run and nowhere to hide! Give her to me or I’ll hunt you down and kill all of you!”

Alice moves the stick into a higher gear and accelerates towards the Mini. The Beast closes in on them with relative ease.

CHAPTER 8
Hope on Hell's Highway

In the driver seat, Johnny is a fixture of unwavering concentration. Georgie stands in fight mode barking out the back windscreen at the oncoming Beast. The Beast is all menace and terror.

Nicole says, "He's gonna crush us! Can't you go any faster?"

Johnny replies, "We're going at full speed!"

The Mini vibrates rapidly and the engine over-revs as it reaches its maximum speed. Still the Beast makes up ground on them. Johnny looks in the driver side mirror but is blinded by the high beam lights of Alice's Beast.

Fire and smoke erupt from the Beast exhaust. Chained to the bulbar, the preacher Danny is inches from being smashed into the Mini. Just before impact Alice activates the exhaust brakes, eliciting a deafening engine roar to slow the Beast. But there is no kindness in Alice's actions. His primary objective is to terrorize them. It is the game that Alice loves. The thrill of the hunt.

"Fuck!" Anna exclaims.

Alice says, “Say your last rights preacher.”

“Not yet!” Johnny asserts as they approach a steep winding part on the highway.

Alice’s truck falls behind as the steep path slows his speed. Alice shifts to a lower gear. The engine makes a loud roar as it pulls the truck up the steep, winding road. Thick fire and black smoke pump out of the truck’s exhaust. The Mini reaches the crest of the hill and goes fast down the other side.

The Beast nears the hills crest. As it passes over the hill, Alice launches the Beast powerfully down at full tilt. Georgie barks with fury at the oncoming truck.

Nicole says, “Here he comes again!”

Johnny says, “He's too fast, I can't clear away from him!”

The Mini is at full speed and the truck still closes to within inches of its rear end. Alice swerves the Beast left and right across the motorway to taunt them.

“Ready for the scrapheap suckers?” Alice says through the radio. “Just pull over and give me the girl. I’ll let the rest of you go free.”

Johnny turns the Mini onto the shoulder of the highway. The Beast follows, keeping tight on their tail.

Johnny pulls the Mini to the other side of the highway. Surprisingly, the Beast follows with ease.

“Shit!” Johnny says, unable to outfox Alice.

“You had your chance…” Alice says.

“No!” shouts Anna.

The Beast engine roars to life as Alice cackles through the radio. Alice’s Beast slams into the back of the Mini, splattering Danny into minced meat. His blood splashes the back windscreen of the Mini, soaking it red.

The Mini spins out of control. Anna screams. The Mini rolls onto its roof and slides along the gravel. Georgie is catapulted out of the vehicle and bounces on the ground. The Mini comes to rest in a ditch off to the side of the highway.

Georgie lay dead still twenty meters from the Mini. Johnny, Nicole, and Anna hang upside down in the Mini. Johnny and Nicole have been knocked unconscious. Anna is mildly concussed.

Alice stops the Beast. The driver side door opens. Alice's big black boots step down from the truck and approach the wreckage of the Mini. Upon reaching the Mini, Alice only has eyes for Anna. She is his reward. He smiles, anticipating the fun to come.

Alice opens the back door of the upturned Mini. Alice pulls the hunting knife from the scabbard of his belt and cuts Anna free of her seatbelt restraint. Anna falls. Alice pulls Anna out of the Mini and drags her to the back of the truck.

Alice lowers the truck tailgate down and drags Anna onto the tailgate. The evil amber eyes of Justice prey upon the intruder. Justice growls, his hunger is overwhelming. Alice rides the tailgate up to the trailer floor. Justice barks ferociously. Alice drags Anna inside the trailer and shuts the rear door of the trailer.

Meanwhile, Officer Rob's patrol car sits idle on the shoulder of the highway by Danny's abandoned combi. Sitting in the driver seat, Rob calls a familiar friend for another favor.

Across the highway at Kruger Scrap Metal Yard, Matt's burnt-out Ute is being lifted by a large claw attached to a crawling crane from a tow truck to a metal crushing machine. Slim, driving the crawling crane, hears his mobile phone ringing out. He stops the crawler, checks caller ID on the mobile and answers.

"I'm just finishin off the last job you sent me" Slim says.

"I've got another one for you" Rob says.

"Our boy bin busy again, has he?"

"Yeah… A combi smooshed in a tree in Dead Valley."

"It's gonna cost ya double"

"Double?"

"This shits gettin too regular."

"What can I do Slim? I owe him one"

"You don't owe him shit! He's a rotten egg. Always has bin. It's time you let that motherfucker take care of his own problems."

"This is the last time"

"That's what you always say Bobby."

"You know what it was like back then, Slim?"

"I don't live in the past mate. I've moved on with my life. You should do the same."

Slim disconnects the call as Rob ponders his fate.

Meanwhile, the upturned wreckage of the Mini lay in a ditch off to the side of the highway.

A weary Johnny helps Nicole scramble out of the Mini.

“He’s taken Anna!” Johnny says.

“What are we to do now?” Nicole replies.

Johnny attempts to push the upturned Mini back onto its wheels. Nicole looks on at Johnny’s futile efforts.

“Help me Nic! I can’t give up! As long as she’s alive we must try to help her.” Johnny says.

Nicole helps Johnny to push the Mini without success. Sensing their predicament is hopeless, Nicole succumbs and sits down.

Nicole says, “It’s hopeless”.

Johnny also slumps on the ground, despondent.

“Where is Georgie?” Johnny asks.

“He was thrown out in the crash.” Nicole responds.

Johnny and Nicole search the surrounding area. Nicole stumbles on Georgie’s body lying in a bush nearby. Georgie is still, his body caked in blood. Nicole says, “Grab a blanket!”

Johnny brings a blanket over from the Mini.

“How is he?” Johnny asks.

Nicole shakes her head.

Johnny cradles Georgie in his arms and wraps him in the blanket.

“Poor Georgie.” Johnny says.

"We're FUBAR now!" Nicole says.

"Not yet!" Johnny says.

"We're in the middle of nowhere with no one nearby. What do you suggest we do?" Nicole replies.

"We need to send out a distress signal. Do you still keep the can of petrol in the trunk?" Johnny asks.

"Yeah, why?" Nicole asks.

"I have an idea" Johnny replies.

Meanwhile, Officer Rob, driving the patrol car along the highway sees an explosion in the distance.

"Dear God!" Rob says.

A plume of smoke rises in the night sky. Rob turns on all the lights and sirens and accelerates towards the source of the explosion.

The Mini is in flames. Thick clouds of smoke are pluming from the burning fuel tank. Nicole looks with melancholy at the Mini inferno. How could Johnny do this to her prized Mini?

Johnny stands across from the Mini inferno holding a can of petrol. He watches the blaze erupt into the night sky.

Officer Rob's patrol car with the lights and sirens blaring approach from the distance.

"Holy moly!" Johnny says. "It's a miracle…"

“It’s a miracle alright” Nicole responds, astounded.

But Nicole is in no mood to congratulate him, with her Mini a burning wreck. The flashing police lights and the burning wreckage of the Mini create an eerily arresting visual. Rob stops the patrol car in front of them and gets out.

Rob says, “Is anyone hurt?”

Johnny says, “Just our dog. Our daughter has been kidnapped by a maniac truck driver!”

Rob responds, “Oh no! Which way did they go?”

Johnny looks at his mobile phone tracker. “They’re a hundred clicks away, heading towards Kruger.”

“Get in my mean machine and buckle up. We’ll catch them in no time!”

Johnny lay Georgie, who is wrapped in a blanket, in the trunk of the patrol car.

Johnny rides shotgun and Nicole gets in the back of the patrol car. Rob’s patrol car takes off down the highway at high speed with the lights flashing.

CHAPTER 9
The Highway Hunter and Anna

The Beast is parked at an abandoned rest area for long haul truckers. Alice, operating the control panel in his prime mover, turns on the CCTV monitor and the internal trailer lights. Anna hangs from chains inside the trailer, with her feet standing timidly on Justice's rusty cage. Justice snaps hungrily at Anna's feet without success. Anna is suspended from the ceiling tracks, her wrists cuffed and chained.

Alice presses the button on the two-way radio handset and speaks. His creepy voice comes through the speakers in the trailer, "I've got a present for you, Justice."

"Keep that fucker away from me!" Anna shouts.

Justice barks viciously.

“All in good time precious” Alice replies.

“Please? Don't do this! I’ll be a good girl” Anna begs.

“I know you are a naughty girl. Justice knows it too. He can smell it on your nasty little cunt.” Alice snarls.

Justice leaps and his teeth graze Anna’s foot, drawing blood. Justice laps up the blood droplets that fall into the cage.

Anna shouts, “Fuck you!”

Alice presses a button on his control panel. The steel spike bolted to the headboard flicks out.

“You shouldn’t have tried to flee.” Alice says.

Alice puts the truck into gear and drives off. The Beast gets up to speed on the highway. Blood drips into the cage. Justice barks, claws, and bites ferociously at Anna's feet, baying for more blood.

Anna shouts, “Leave me alone!”

Anna's foot slips off the cage, leaving her to suspend freely from the chains.

Alice fires up the Beast. Fire and smoke blow out of the twin exhausts as the Beast goes full tilt ahead. Alice looks to the CCTV screen and says into the two-way, “Little birdy, can you fly?”

Anna cries out in anticipation. Alice braces tightly on the steering wheel and activates the truck and trailer brakes. The twenty-two-wheels burn rubber on the highway, forcing the Beast to a sudden stop. Anna is propelled powerfully forward towards the ominous looking steel spike.

Terrified, she screams out, “Nooo!”

At the final moment before impact with the steel spike, Anna pulls hard at the chains and thrusts her legs out in front. Her feet come up and she extends her legs out either side of the steel spike. The steel spike narrowly misses her groin. Anna’s feet push off the headboard and she slide backwards away from the spike. Anna comes to a stop halfway down the trailer. She breathes a big sigh of relief.

Alice watches the CCTV monitor with an air of surprised satisfaction. This young girl has fighting spirit. She is nothing like what he had expected from their first meeting. She has a vigor and fight to live like no other he has hunted before.

Alice says, "You're so very clever little birdy! There's hope for you yet!"

Alice wants a closer look at his prized little birdy. Usually, Alice would wait until he reaches the watering hole to unleash his inner beast. But today his impulses are getting the better of him. His craving for the sweet and sexy Anna is too strong to be restrained or controlled. He must have a taste to quench his thirst right now.

The hydraulic tailgate comes up to trailer height. The imposing presence of the Highway Hunter stands ominously on the tailgate with knife in hand. He shuffles inside the trailer. Justice sits obediently in his rusty cage watching his master.

"Mmm! Sweet and sour. My favorite scent", Alice says.

Anna hangs tiredly from the chains with her head slumped over her chest. Anna can hear Alice's breathing increase in volume as he approaches, until he stands directly opposite her, staring into her soul. Alice grabs Anna by the nape of her neck and pulls her head up so that she is face to face with him.

Anna opens her eyes and spits in his face. Alice licks the spit from his face. Alice kisses Anna on the lips. She turns her head away in disgust.

"I'd rather die!" Anna shouts.

Alice says, "If you insist."

Alice holds the knife out threateningly in front of Anna's face. He pulls Anna's singlet out near her midriff and cuts it upwards towards her busty breasts. The blade slices her tummy, drawing blood.

“Aaagh!” Anna cries out.

A fury flows through Anna just as fierce as when Karen and her clique forced her head into the sullied toilet water. Anna unleashes her inner beast. She sticks her neck out and bites viciously into Alice's right ear, tearing out a chunk of flesh.

“Oww!” Alice shouts.

Blood spills onto the trailer floor. Anna spits the chunk of flesh onto the trailer floor. Justice sniffs hungrily for the fresh chunk of ear.

“You bitch!” Alice shouts.

With her mouth filled with blood, Anna grins. Alice presses the sharp tip of the knife into Anna's throat, piercing the skin and drawing blood.

Alice says, “It’s time for you to see what happens to those who provoke me”.

CHAPTER 10
Tighter and Tighter

Rob's police car goes at full tilt on the highway, reaching speeds of 250 km/hr. The police lights glow blue and red in the desert darkness.

Johnny looks at his mobile GPS app tracking Anna's phone.

"They are close!" Johnny says. He continues, "They aren't moving! Why would they stop?"

"He may have found the phone and threw it away, or…" Rob says, pausing and looking over to Johnny with a worried expression.

“Or what?” Johnny asks.

“Or your daughters met with foul play”

Johnny looks at his mobile tracker. Johnny says, “We’re right on top of them now! Can you see Anna?”

“Up ahead!” Nicole shouts.

“I see” Rob says.

The Beast is parked on the shoulder of the highway a kilometer away.

Officer Rob turns off the police lights and drives quietly up to the Beast in neutral, the element of surprise in his favor. There is a light coming from inside the trailer.

Rob stops the police car directly behind the truck.

Rob grabs Johnny by the arm.

“Follow my lead.” Rob says, continuing, “Don’t do anything stupid!”

Rob approaches the rear of the trailer with Johnny in tow.

Rob shouts, “Police! Come out with your hands raised!”

Consumed by his desire for the girl, Alice has exposed himself to capture. Alice acts swiftly to escape his quandary. Alice slips underneath the trailer through a trap door in the floor and creeps back to the prime mover. Alice starts the engine of the Beast.

Johnny shouts, “Up front!” and runs towards the prime mover.

Officer Rob shouts, “Stop!”

Alice puts the Beast into gear and gets the truck moving.

Johnny shouts, “Shit! Shit! They’re getting away!”

Rob shouts, “Come back!”

Johnny catches up to and leaps up the stairs of the prime mover as Alice changes gears and increases the Beast’s speed. Johnny reaches into the driver side window and grabs Alice around the collar.

“Where is Anna?” Johnny shouts.

Alice takes his right hand off the steering wheel and elbows Johnny hard in the face. Johnny falls backwards. He reaches out to grab onto the driver side mirror. Alice accelerates. Johnny stumbles and loses his footing to hang freely from the driver side mirror.

The patrol car with all the lights and siren blaring accelerates after Alice’s Beast.

Hanging by the driver side mirror, Johnny extends his foot out and gets footing back on the step. Johnny reaches though the window and grabs Alice by the collar.

“Where is she?” Johnny asks.

Alice draws his head back, pulling Johnny inwards and then he head-butts Johnny hard in the nose. Johnny’s nose smashes. He falls off the step down to the ground. As his torso hits the road Johnny wraps his arm around the inside of the step. Johnny’s legs and torso and drag along the road, tearing the skin off his leg. Johnny extends his feet out and the road burns through the rubber soles of his shoes. Still, Alice accelerates.

“Stop him!” Nicole shouts.

Rob’s patrol car is directly behind Alice’s truck. Rob speeds up to overtake Alice’s truck on the right. Alice steers right to cut them off.

Rob accelerates to overtake on the left-hand side, but Alice swerves left to cut him off. Johnny gets dragged under the truck.

“No! No!” Nicole shouts, thinking Johnny is dead and gone.

But Johnny maintains his grip with both hands and feet on the underside of the prime mover. Johnny grabs onto the chassis and pulls himself up between the prime mover and trailer.

Rob accelerates the patrol car to over-take the Beast on the right. Alice swerves right and Rob adapts, accelerating to the left-hand side, speeding alongside the Beast, and over taking it.

Alice slams the Beast into the backside of the patrol car, smashing off the car’s back bumper bar. It falls onto the road and Alice drives over the top of it.

“Aagh!”, Nicole screams.

Johnny kneels on the chassis in between the prime mover and trailer. Johnny pulls out the air supply cables causing air to expel freely. The brakes of the trailer lock up, retarding the Beast. The prime mover drags the trailer along the highway, burning all the tread off the trailer tires. The

Beast slows down considerably.

"FUCK!" Alice shouts.

Johnny opens the passenger door of the Beast and gets in.

Johnny says, "Where is Anna? What have you done with her?"

Alice grins sadistically at Johnny, replying "Who?"

Johnny searches the driver cab for Anna but there is no sign of her.

"She ain't in 'ere!" shouts Alice, and slams Johnny in the nose with his free forearm. Blood spills from Johnny's nose. Johnny grabs Alice around the throat and the two men wrestle for control of the truck.

Johnny pulls the trailer brake, and the Beast comes to an abrupt stop.

The hulking Alice opens the driver door. Alice grabs Johnny forcefully with both hands and tosses him out of the truck like a ragdoll. Johnny falls heavily to the ground. The bulky bull of a man shuffles down the stairs and over to Johnny. Alice grabs Johnny by the hair and pulls his head back, exposing his throat. Alice takes out his hunting knife.

"Time for you to join your little girl" Alice says.

Officer Rob, with his gun aimed at Alice's back, shouts, "Stop! Drop the knife and let him go!!"

Alice begrudgingly does as he is told.

"Put your hands on your head and kneel," Officer Rob says.

Alice obeys Rob's command.

Johnny grabs Alice and shouts, "Anna's in the trailer, isn't she?"

Alice smiles at Johnny, then says, "Pretty little thing, isn't she?"

Johnny punches Alice hard in the face. Alice's jaw snaps back from the blow.

"Back off Johnny!" Rob says.

"Check the trailer!" Johnny says. "I bet Anna is in there!"

Rob says to Alice, "Buddy, I'm going to have to search your trailer."

"Do you have a warrant?" Alice asks.

"Open it"

"Whatever you say Officer."

Officer Rob escorts Alice to the back of the trailer. Johnny follows.

Alice, operating a control panel at the rear of the trailer, drops the hydraulic tailgate down. Rob shines his torch inside the trailer. Justice growls from within his rusty cage, unhappy that his rest has been disturbed.

"That's a vicious looking dog!" Rob says.

"It isn't a crime to own a guard dog, is it officer?" Alice responds.

"No."

"What have you done with Anna?" Johnny asks.

"Who?" Alice replies.

"Where is my daughter?" Johnny shouts.

Alice says, "I don't know what you're going on about buddy. Have a look for yourself. There's no girl in there."

Johnny climbs up onto the trailer floor.

Alice rebukes, "He can't go in there!"

Rob says, "Yes he can! If you've got nothing to hide you've got nothing to worry about."

Alice approaches Rob and says, "This is bullshit! You're making this shit up!"

Rob draws his gun and says, "Get on your knees and put your hands behind your head!"

Alice replies, "Ok" and does as Rob orders with deliberate slowness.

Johnny walks passed Justice's rusty cage. Justice barks madly and slams into the cage door. How dare this man come through Justice's turf? This man must die! Justice rocks against the rusty cage, almost snapping the metal fixtures holding the cage onto the trailer floor.

Johnny reaches the front of the trailer. Johnny is surprised at just how short the trailer length seems inside. It must be five to ten meters shorter than the outside. Also, even though the reefer motor is powering outside, there is no cold air coming through inside the trailer.

The hydraulic tailgate begins to close. Johnny rushes to the back of the trailer as the light dims. The tailgate closes, locking Johnny inside darkness. Johnny bangs on the tailgate door with both fists.

"Hey! What's going on?" Johnny shouts.

Outside the trailer, Alice approaches his old friend. Smiling, he says, "Blu… Blu…Blubbering Bobby... my savior."

Rob, stands up by the tailgate controls and says, "Again Alice? You've got to stop this!"

Alice accosts Bobby and places his hand on his chest. "Don't ever tell me to stop Bobby" Alice says.

"You're out of control!" Bobby says, "I can't keep covering for you!"

"Who was there for you when that priest got the touchy feelies for your ass? It'll stop when I say it stops, Blu… Blu… Blubber Boy!"

"Stop it, Alice! I don't stutter anymore."

"You think because you're cured of your stutter that you're too good for me now."

"What do you plan to do with them?"

"Justice will feed on the man. The girl belongs to me."

"I won't let that happen! I've let you get away with this for too long."

“Are you going to stop me boy?”

“I’ll do whatever it takes!”

Alice takes a remote-control device from his jacket pocket. Alice continues, “It’s Justice’s feeding time! Try and stop me from releasing him…”

Bobby reaches out and wrestles Alice for control of the device. Bobby pleads, “Give it to me, Alice.”

The bulky bull of a man shoves Bobby away with considerable ease. “Pathetic”, Alice says, then presses a button on the device.

Inside the trailer, there is an electronic sound, and the gate of Justice’s rusty cage slides open. Evil amber eyes fix on Johnny, who stands at the rear of the trailer. Justice crawls out of his cage.

“Oh shit!” Johnny says. Johnny faces the predator with seemingly no chance of escape. Justice growls and bares his sharp teeth as he prepares to attack. Johnny scans his surroundings. Above Johnny two chains hang down from the ceiling. Johnny jumps up to one of the chains and grabs it with both hands.

A snarling Justice bounces off his hind legs to attack Johnny. Holding the chain, Johnny kicks off the tailgate door and slides forward along the ceiling tracking. Justice launches at Johnny and his claws scratch through Johnny’s pants bottom as he passes underneath him. Justice slams hard into the steel tailgate wall. He rolls around on the floor, winded and struggling for breath.

Johnny slides to the front, where he lets go of the chain and drops onto the trailer floor. Johnny knocks on the wall repeatedly with his fists. It makes a hollow sound. Johnny shouts, "Anna? Are you back there?"

Obstructed, weak cries for help comes from beyond the wall. Johnny puts the side of his head up against the wall. He can clearly hear Anna's muffled cry for help. Johnny carefully scans the wall for an entry point.

Having had a chance to recover, Justice is now angrier than ever. Justice growls like a rabid beast, then fixes his evil, amber eyes on Johnny. The man must die! Justice bounces towards Johnny to resume his attack.

Johnny sees a button on the wall. He presses the small button. A door opens and foggy, cold air spews out. Justice launches into the air at Johnny to attack with his mouth open wide.

Johnny quickly enters the secret cold room and shuts the door. Justice slams into the wall hard, almost buckling it with the force of his weight. Justice cries out, more from wounded pride than actual injury. The man bettered him, and Justice isn't accustomed to losing.

Johnny shivers from the extreme cold as his eyes adjust in the foggy, dark room.

Once his eyes have adjusted, Johnny exclaims, "Oh my god!"

The heads of the Highway Hunter's victims are mounted to the front wall. Alice calls this his 'Head-Board'. Each head is a trophy from the Highway Hunter's killing ritual.

Anna hangs from the ceiling with her wrists chained together over a hook.

Johnny rushes over to her aid.

Johnny grabs Anna around the torso and raises her up, lifting her wrists off the hook. Johnny gently lays Anna down onto the trailer floor.

“Anna! Are you ok?” Johnny shouts.

Anna is unresponsive. Johnny hugs her and rubs her body to warm her up. Johnny slaps Anna’s cheek.

“Anna! Anna!” Johnny shouts.

Anna opens her eyes tiredly. “Daddy? Is that you?” Anna asks weakly.

“Yes darling.”

“You came for me…”

“Of course! Thank God you’re alive!” Johnny says.

Meanwhile, from the police car, Nicole is now aware of Rob and Alice’s friendship.

“Oh No! They’re in it together!” Nicole says anxiously.

She starts the ignition. Nicole puts the police car into gear and makes for a quick escape.

Bobby turns to the source of the engine starting.

Bobby shouts, “Fuck, she’s gonna get away!”

Alice swiftly pulls the gun from Bobby’s holster.

“No!”, shouts Bobby, reaching for the weapon.

“No loose ends!” replies Alice. He puts his free hand on Bobby’s chest and pushes him backwards.

Nicole, who is getting away in the patrol car, looks nervously in the rear-view mirror.

Alice fires off several rounds. Two bullets pierce the rear screen of the police car. A bullet pierces the back of Nicole’s neck, severing her spinal cord and killing her instantly. Nicole’s head slumps into the driver side door. The patrol car rolls off to the side of the road, comes to rest against a rock and stalls.

“Give me my gun back!” Bobby shouts, reaching for his gun.

“No!” Alice replies.

“Give it Alice!”

The two men wrestle for control of the weapon. Alice fires off three rounds that hit Bobby in the chest. Bobby stumbles backwards and collapses to the ground. He looks up at Alice with a startled expression.

“You gave me no choice Bobby.” Alice says.

Blood soaks Bobby’s shirt from the gunshot wounds. His dead eyes stare blankly into the night sky.

Alice walks over to the reefer unit at the front of the trailer. The temperature gauge sits on zero degrees Celsius. Alice turns the temperature down to minus twenty-eight degrees Celsius.

Freezing cold, foggy air spews out of the reefer unit into the cold room.

“I’m freezing” Anna says through chattering teeth.

“Oh shit! It’s getting much colder! We must escape now!” Johnny says.

Johnny rushes over and opens the door he came through. Justice barks viciously and snaps at him from the other side of the door. Johnny shuts the door.

Anna loses consciousness. Johnny rushes back to Anna and wraps her tightly in his embrace.

“There’s no way out!” Johnny says franticly, as the freezing cold air drops Anna’s body temperature to dangerous levels.

Anna’s whole body feels cold, and she shivers uncontrollably. Her blood pressure increases, and she passes out.

“Anna! Stay with me darling!” Johnny shouts as he tries to keep Anna conscious. But it is too late. And now, Johnny starts to feel drowsy and confused. His body temperature also drops below safe levels.

The door opens and the large bulky figure of Alice walks into the room. Slipping in and out of consciousness, Johnny looks towards the large bulk of a man. Alice looks down on Johnny and smiles. Now the real fun begins. Johnny passes out.

CHAPTER 11
Bait and Switch

Alice splashes water in Anna's face. She awakens disorientated yet relieved to be alive. But her relief vanishes as she gathers her senses. She sits in the driver's seat of the Beast with Alice riding shotgun.

Alice says, "Ok little birdy, I'm gonna teach you to drive my Beast. Are you ready?"

"Fuck you!" Anna replies.

"Here, I'll make it easy for you." Alice says, switching the transmission lever from 'Manual' to 'Automatic'.

"I'm not doing your dirty work!"

"Ah…" Alice says, continuing, "You need some extra motivation."

Alice turns on the CCTV monitor. Johnny is suspended from the ceiling by chains in the trailer. His head is slumped down and he is unconscious. Justice is baying for Johnny's blood. He barks viciously from inside his cage, ripping and tearing at the cage doors.

Anna pleads, "No! Let him go!"

Alice replies, "I'm afraid I can't do that"

"Please! It's me you want!"

"Pass my test and I'll let him live."

"How can I be sure that you won't kill him anyway?"

Alice pulls out the hunting knife from the scabbard of his belt and holds it up threateningly to Anna.

Alice snarls, "You don't."

Anna says, "Why are you doing this?"

Alice replies, "Because I hear your sweet voice calling to me." Brandishing the knife Alice says, "Drive or die little birdy"

Anna reluctantly presses the accelerator, and the Beast slowly takes off, switching up a couple of gears.

Inside the trailer, Johnny slowly raises his head. He is weak and incapacitated.

Alice says into the two-way radio, "Welcome back, sleepyhead."

Johnny asks weakly, "Anna… Where is Anna?"

Alice replies, "She's here, driving the Beast."

Mustering all the energy he has left, Johnny shouts, "Stop this! Let Anna go!"

Anna presses the brakes.

Pressing the knife up against Anna's throat, Alice says, "Speed up or I'll kill the both of you."

Anna reluctantly puts her foot down on the accelerator. The truck expels fire and smoke out of the exhaust as it gathers speed, automatically switching up a few gears.

Alice says, “Faster! Feel the power of the Beast!”

Johnny is being thrown around with the momentum of the truck. Much to Alice’s delight, Anna accelerates hard. The Beast switches up another couple of gears.

“Is that fast enough for you?” Anna asks.

“Yes! Very good…We’re flying now.” Alice says.

Alice presses a button on the control panel and the steel spike flicks out from the front wall of the trailer.

“No! What are you doing?” Anna asks.

Alice puts his hand on the trailer brake lever.

Alice says, “It’s time for your daddy to fly away.”

Anna shouts, “No! Don’t do it!”

Alice smiles sadistically. Anna has little time to react. She takes her foot off the accelerator just as Alice pulls hard on the trailer brake lever.

“NOOO!” Anna screams, bracing the steering wheel.

The trailer tires burn rubber and screech as the Beast comes to a sudden stop.

Johnny is propelled forward with the sudden break in momentum.

“Aagh!”, Johnny shouts, looking ominously forwards as his body is thrust towards the steel spike.

The steel spike spears Johnny through the chest with dramatic force. The tip of the spike goes all the way through Johnny’s chest cavity, though bone and tissue, and pierces out of Johnny’s back. Blood spills from Johnny’s mouth. His head slumps down and he stops breathing.

Anna cries out, “NOO! DADDY!”

Justice salivates and growls viciously for the freshly killed meat.

Alice presses a button on the control panel.

Justice’s cage door opens. Justice springs from the cage and launches at Johnny. He tears Johnny to pieces, ripping him off the steel spike and hungrily eating him on the trailer floor.

Alice says, “Congratulations! You’ve passed the test!”

“You miserable fucking cunt!” Anna shouts, hammering her fists into Alice’s chest and clawing at his face.

Alice grabs hold of Anna by the shoulders to subdue her.

Furious with anger, Anna breaks free from his grip and scratches deeply into Alice’s face.

“Aagh!” Alice says, wincing in pain.

Blood trickles down from Alice’s facial wound. Alice grabs Anna by the throat and pushes her head up against the door. With his free hand Alice holds his knife up in a threatening manner.

“Behave! Behave, or I will slit your throat…” Alice says.

“Do it! Your threats don’t scare me anymore! Kill me!” Anna shouts.

“Don’t you want to know what happened to the others?”

“Georgie and Nicole. Where are they?” Anna asks.

Alice says, “I will take you to them.”

“You lie. They are surely dead.”

“No, they are alive. Do you want to see them again?”

“Yes.”

“Drive. I will lead you the way. But first, we must clean out the Beast.”

Dark clouds, thunder and lightning strike the night sky.

Rain begins to fall. The Beast cruises along the highway in darkness.

“Turn left up ahead”, Alice says.

Anna turns the Beast from the highway onto an isolated dirt road. Trees overhang from both sides of the dirt road.

The disused road is bumpy with lots of potholes, which make it hazardous and rough for the truck’s suspension. Anna holds tightly to the steering wheel as the truck bounces up and down. The front steer tire directly under Alice goes over a large pothole, and Alice bounces off his seat, banging his head into the ceiling.

“Aaagh! Watch the road!” Alice says.

Anna can’t help but laugh at Alice’s expense.

The Beast comes out from the dirt track lined by trees to a large open field. The field leads to an embankment which slopes down to a watering hole. Anna drives the Beast through the field.

“Now turn around and reverse down the embankment into the watering hole” Alice instructs.

Little does Alice know that Anna’s trucker dad has taught her some skills. Anna does a looping U-turn and straightens the truck. Effortlessly, she reverses straight down the embankment and stops at the water’s edge next to a giant Elm Tree.

“You’re full of surprises.” Alice says, looking at Anna with reverence. Alice continues, “Now, slowly reverse into the water.”

“Where are Georgie and Nicole?” Anna asks.

“Patience, Little Birdy. Firstly, we must clean the Beast.”

“D’you want me to drive into the water?”

“Yeah, but just the trailer. Not the prime mover.” Alice says.

Anna reverses the Beast. The trailer tires go into the water.

“Steady!” Alice says.

Alice, operating the control panel, lowers the tailgate down into the water. Justice is wise to what is going on. A wary Justice creeps to the front of the trailer to avoid the incoming water.

The water laps over Justice's paws. The incoming water fuels Justice's anxiety. Justice whines. He hates bath time. Justice rushes to the front corner of the trailer, squats down on his haunches and squeezes out a poo.

The trailer goes deeper into the watering hole. Johnny's bloody entrails float on the water's surface.

"Stop! That'll do!", Alice says, as the rear tires of the prime mover reach the water's edge.

But Anna knows she will not get a better opportunity to scupper Alice's plans. So, Anna presses the accelerator down. Hard. The truck reverses into the water until the prime mover tires spin in the mud and the trailer tires are bogged down deep in the hole.

"Noo!" shouts Alice. "Stupid bitch!"

Anna smiles coyly. "Sorry", she says.

"Don't play the fool!", Alice shouts, before continuing, "Drive forward!"

Anna puts the truck into 'low gear' and accelerates. The wheels of the prime mover spin in the mud, unable to get enough traction to drag out the bogged trailer.

Alice looks out the passenger window as the Beast's wheels spin in the mud. With his back to her, Anna opens the driver door and jumps out of the truck. She lands in knee deep water.

“Nooo!” Alice shouts.

Alice jumps out of the driver side door into the watering hole.

Anna gets out of the watering hole and rushes up the embankment.

Rain pours down. A lightning strike hits the elm tree, sparks fly, and a large branch falls in front of Anna, blocking her path.

Alice rushes over and grabs Anna by the hair.

“This is a fine mess you’ve gotten us into!” Alice says.

“Fuck you!” Anna replies.

He drags Anna like a rag doll back into the watering hole.

“Where is Georgie and Nicole?” Anna asks.

“They’re both dead! And you’re about to join them!” Alice replies.

Alice drags Anna to the back of the truck. Anna fights tooth and nail against Alice, clawing and scratching at his face and chest. But he is too big and strong. The rain continues to pelt down as Alice drags Anna through the watering hole.

To Alice’s delight, Anna’s top is soaked in the water, exposing the nipples of her bountiful bosoms. He must have a taste. He forcibly drags her onto the tailgate.

“Let me go!” Anna shouts.

Alice kisses Anna on the lips. She turns her head away.

The rain falls heavily. Lightning flashes. The bright light generated by the lightning exposes Alice's fury at Anna's rejection of him.

Alice pushes Anna's head under water with one of his big hands. Anna thrashes and scratches at Alice's chest as she struggles for air. But it is of little use. Alice is just too powerful for her to overcome physically.

Alice raises Anna's head above the water's surface and kisses her. Anna turns her head away, rejecting Alice.

"It's a shame it has to end this way little birdy" Alice says, and he pushes Anna's head back underwater. Alice forcibly holds Anna's head underwater. Anna struggles with all her might, reaching up with her right arm and scratching Alice's chest. But Alice merely shrugs off the scratching. The life drains out of Anna and her body goes limp.

But Alice still wants to keep Anna alive. He had lots of plans for them. If she dies right now, it will spoil his fun. It cannot end this way, so soon.

Alice pulls Anna's head above water. Anna gathers her breath back, gasping for oxygen.

Alice says, "Stop resisting and I'll let you live!"

Once Anna gets her breath back, Alice kisses her. Anna kisses him back. Finally, Alice thinks to himself. Alice tears off Anna's top, exposing her bountiful bosoms.

Anna puts her hand on Alice's chest and says, "Let me get on top!". Alice lets Anna straddle on top of him, her big boobs soaking wet. Alice voraciously grabs at Anna's breasts, sucking the nipples. Anna puts her head back and moans in pleasure.

But Anna is merely pretending to be aroused. Anna hugs Alice and caresses his burly shoulders. Alice tears off Anna's pants, exposing her bum. Alice can barely contain his excitement. With Alice distracted in ravaging her body, Anna reaches behind Alice's back and grabs the hunting knife from the scabbard of his belt.

Anna seizes her opportunity. She drives the sharp blade into the back of Alice's neck. The knife penetrates deeply. Alice's eyes go wide, and he screams out in pain.

Anna withdraws the knife. Blood sprays from Alice's wound. Anna stabs at Alice again. Alice deflects the knife away and shoves Anna off him. Anna falls into the water.

Alice reaches for his stab wound and his hand comes away bloodied. Anna comes back at Alice with the knife.

In a frenzied attack she slices and dices at Alice, who takes most of the knife wounds on his forearms. Anna is unleashing her fury with merciless intent. Alice turns his back and retreats to the trailer. Anna lunges with the knife and stabs the blade into Alice's back. Alice falls forward onto the trailer floor with the knife stuck in his back.

Alice reaches behind his back to retrieve the knife, but he cannot remove it from his back.

"You bitch!" Alice screams.

"Time for you to receive your justice!" Anna says.

Anna presses a button on the tailgate control panel.

"No!" screams Alice, as the tailgate door closes, locking him inside.

Justice advances through the sullied water towards Alice, stalking him. Justice growls his vicious intent.

Alice says, "Stay Justice. Heel!"

Justice is immersed in the water, his amber eyes fixed on Alice. Baring his teeth, he is hungry for blood and Alice is on the menu.

"No, Justice! No, please!" Alice pleads.

Justice launches at Alice.

"Aagh!" screams Alice.

Anna hears Alice's screams and the crunching and ripping of flesh from bone, as Alice's cries for mercy are ignored by Justice.

As Alice's cries die out the rainfall starts to subside. Stark-naked and drenched to the bone, Anna wades through the water.

With the trailer being bogged deep in the hole, there is no retrieving it without assistance from heavy equipment. Anna figures if she can disconnect the truck from the trailer, she should be able to drive the prime mover out of the hole.

Anna disconnects the truck air supply plugs from the trailer. She pulls the release handle on the turntable to disconnect the truck from the trailer.

Anna climbs into the prime mover and starts the engine. The Beast roars to life. Anna revs the engine and smoke fires from the twin exhaust pipes. She shifts the Beast into a low gear and presses on the accelerator. The steer tires spin in the mud, unable to get any traction, and the Beast stays still.

Anna presses a button to lock the diffs of the drive axles. She tries again, applying steady pressure on the accelerator pedal. This time the Beast rolls slowly forward, the tires finding traction on rocks beneath the muddy ground. The prime mover disengages from the trailer. The trailer topples over front first, sinking to the floor of the watering hole.

Anna drives the truck out of the watering hole. Smoke fires out from the twin exhausts as Anna accelerates the Beast up the embankment, through the field and back along the dirt track.

In the rearview mirror Anna sees Alice's black trailer lying in its final resting place. Good riddance. Let it rot, along with Alice and Justice.

Anna drives along the dirt track back to the highway. There she meets a fork in the road. She can turn left and return home to where she came from. Or she can turn right and drive to Kruger where her mother is. Anna's old home stopped feeling like a home when Charlie died. And now there is nothing waiting for her there but painful memories.

Anna accelerates the truck towards Kruger. Her mother is all the family she has got left. Anna is exhausted, both physically and emotionally, but feels euphoria in her triumph over Alice. She beat the Highway Hunter where others failed. She feels a sense of relief it is all over.

Anna drives the Beast passed Bobby's patrol car and pulls over to investigate. Bobby lay dead on the ground with three bullets in his chest. Nicole is slumped dead in the driver seat with a bullet hole in her neck. Fearing there is only death to be found here, Anna turns around to return to the truck. That's when she hears scratching noises coming from the trunk.

She approaches and hears a high-pitched doggy whimper. Anna pops the trunk of the car. Georgie leaps up at her excitedly with the white blanket hanging off him.

"Georgie!" Anna says excitedly. Georgie barks his excitement to see Anna. Georgie jumps up and puts his paws on Anna's chest, licking her neck and face. Anna pats Georgie's tummy, feeling around for any damage, but he is fine.

"It's great to see you, Georgie!" Anna says, continuing, "Let's get out of 'ere!"

Anna walks back to the truck. Georgie jumps out of the trunk and follows her. Anna lifts Georgie into the truck.

Anna accelerates the truck down the highway with smoke blowing from the twin exhaust pipes. A sign off to the side of the highway reads 'Welcome to Kruger- our dreamy little town'.

END.

HIGHWAY HUNTER by Richard Chappell

Printed in Great Britain
by Amazon